# The Sweetheart Hoax

Christy Hayes

ISBN: 1477633510
ISBN-13: 978-1477633519

# DEDICATION

To readers everywhere. Thank you!

# OTHER BOOKS BY CHRISTY HAYES

Angle of Incidence

Dodge the Bullet

Heart of Glass

Misconception

Shoe Strings

The Accidental Encore

Golden Rule Outfitters Series:
Mending the Line, Book 1
Guiding the Fall, Book 2
Taming the Moguls, Book 3

Maybe it's You
Formula for a Perfect Life
Stalling for Time
The End Run

# ACKNOWLEDGMENTS

To my family for their love and support, always.

# CHAPTER 1

Margot Manning had to quit the job she loved in order to achieve the career she wanted. As she settled into her chair at the reception desk at Flannery & Williams, she wondered what could have made the last few years worse. She could have been waiting tables at a diner as her mother had done before her heart made such physical work too taxing. She could have hawked gifts at one of the coastal area's gift stores, unable to study without her bosses or customers taking note. She could have accepted one of the nannying positions she'd interviewed for before realizing she'd never be able to read and memorize chapters of organic chemistry with toddlers underfoot all day. As she neared the end of her part-time nursing program, she knew she'd made the right choice for her day job. If only she hadn't fallen stupidly, ignorantly in love with her boss...well, one of them.

Phil Williams was cocky, handsome, and obscenely talented. Flannery & Williams was the hottest environmental architectural and building firm in the Lowcountry, and Phil and his insatiable drive to succeed had put them on the map. She didn't need a distraction like him in her life; she sure as hell wasn't looking for one when she'd accepted the job three years ago. The receptionist's position had been the perfect chance for her to work in a job that required minimum skill and left plenty of time for her to study. The fact that her two bosses were the best looking men in South Carolina was just a perk. A perk that quickly turned into a liability when awe and infatuation morphed slowly, achingly, into unrequited love.

"Morning, Margot," Phil said as he breezed past her on the way to his office. He plopped a bag on her desk from his favorite bakery. His thick, dark hair and caramel colored eyes perfectly complemented the beige suite and blue shirt he'd chosen that morning. As usual, he hadn't even made eye contact.

Margot jumped up from her chair. "Phil, I need to speak with you for a minute."

"Can't," he said without a backwards glance. "I've got an appointment in thirty minutes."

Margot moved the bag and cleared away her National Council Licensure Examination study guide in order to skim the calendar. She trailed behind him and stopped at the threshold of his door. "I didn't know you had an appointment."

He slid out of his suit coat and draped it over the wooden hanger in the corner. "Made it last night at the driving range. I'll need a promotional package and complete set up in the conference room."

Margot blew one of her flyaway curls out of her eyes. Unfortunately, it sounded like a sigh.

"Too tall an order?" he asked with a sideways grin, looking at her for the first time as he sat in his chair.

Everything about Phil Williams was a very tall order. At six-foot-four, he stood exactly a foot higher than Margot. "No, of course not."

"Good."

When she didn't leave or even stand up straight where she'd slumped against the door, he spared her another glance.

"I do need to talk to you," she said as he raised his brows. "Later."

"Fine, but I've got a lunch date, so it'll have to be this afternoon."

"That's..." typical, she wanted to say, "perfect." She stood up straight. "Thanks for breakfast."

She skulked down the hallway toward the conference room, grabbed the pitcher from the cabinet, and retrieved a lemon from the small refrigerator under the sink. She sliced the lemon and muttered all the reasons she shouldn't care that he had another lunch date. Of course he had a lunch date. God knew he wouldn't have had that charming glow in his eye just for the anticipation of seeing her first thing in the morning. She added ice and water from the tap, set out the nice glasses on the bamboo tray, and went back to the wet bar for the bowl of chocolate candies.

At least when she quit, she wouldn't have to know the details of his love life. She wouldn't have to go home at night picturing him dining with unworthy women at Andover's best restaurants under reservations she'd made. Soon, she told herself, very soon, she wouldn't care who Phil Williams bought breakfast for or what he did for lunch or dinner and with whom. She'd be too busy to care and way too happy. Nursing was all she'd ever wanted to do, and through sheer determination and hard work, her goal was finally within sight.

Now all she had to do was quit her job.

***

When the phone rang for the third time and Phil heard Margot puttering around the conference room, he answered it himself, a little distracted by his upcoming meeting and the fact that he'd seen his lunch date's picture on a billboard on his ride into the office that morning.

"Flannery & Williams. Phil speaking."

The sound of his mother's voice on the other end did little to settle his mood. "You're answering your own phone? I thought you had a secretary for that."

"Mom. How nice to hear from you." He glanced at his watch. He didn't have time to play twenty questions with an important meeting in fifteen minutes.

"If that were true, you'd call me more often. Since you don't, I'm forced to bother you at work." He heard the telltale sign she had breakfast on the stove as the sound of bacon popping filled his ear. "So how are you?"

"Busy," he said. "I've got a meeting in a few minutes I need to prepare for."

3

"Busy, busy, busy. I never heard back from you about your daddy's retirement party. We're three weeks out, so I'm calling to remind you to book a flight before the prices go sky high. Delta's running a special out of Charleston."

Damn. He hadn't forgotten about the party. Not really. He just didn't want to go. "I've got it on my calendar to book this week."

"Good," she said. "Will anyone be joining you for the party?"

"Anyone like whom? You mean a date?"

"Phillip, you're thirty-one years old, not married, and not in a relationship. I should have grandchildren by now."

"You have grandchildren. I'm sure Devon would be thrilled to hear you've forgotten his kids."

"I mean grandchildren from you. Aren't you the least bit embarrassed that your younger brother is married with two kids? People are starting to talk."

"Talk about what? People in Cash are always talking."

"I didn't want to tell you this over the phone, but your brother said there are rumors you might be gay."

"What?" Phil sputtered and ran his hand through his hair, and then mentally cursed when he realized he'd mussed it up. "Are you serious?"

"You ran off to a resort island, you never come home, and whenever you do, you're alone." He heard the sound of her spatula against cast iron. "It didn't help when you wore a purple shirt last Thanksgiving."

"It was plum! And everyone was wearing purple last season."

"I rest my case," she mumbled under her breath. "Honey, I think I'd know if you were that way, but you can't blame people for wondering."

He shouldn't care what people in Cash, Illinois thought of him. He certainly hadn't given anyone from his hometown a second thought in years. But gay? The thought made him shudder. "I'm not gay, Mom. For God's sake, ask Julianne how gay I am."

"Phillip Williams, I most certainly will not ask Julianne Waterston anything of the sort."

"She wasn't Julianne Waterston when she let me—" Good Lord, was he seriously about to tell his mother he'd had sex with the preacher's daughter in high school? "It doesn't matter because I won't be alone on this trip."

"Really?" she all but purred. "Is it serious?"

Seriously stupid, yes. Who the hell could he bring home to get his mother and all the wagging tongues in Cash off his back? "It's working toward serious. I wasn't going to ask her to come, but since you and everyone else need some proof of my manhood, I'm sure she won't mind tagging along."

"Well, hot diggity dog. Wait 'til I tell your brother."

Great. For all he knew, she'd put an ad in the Cash Courier. "I've got to go, Mom. My meeting's about to start."

"Wait," she pleaded. "What's her name? What does she look like? Where's she from?"

"I'll call you with the flight details. Tell Dad I'll be there."

"You're going to leave me guessing?"

He was going to leave her exactly where he found himself: with absolutely no idea who he was bringing home to meet his mother.

# CHAPTER 2

"What are you doing?" Bo Williams asked his wife.

Judy whipped her head up and unclasped her hands. "What do you mean?"

Bo sniffed the air and gaped at the bacon lying on a pile of paper towels. "You made bacon?"

"Yeah," Judy said. "So what?" She hopped up and reached for a plate from the cabinet. She placed three slices on his plate and slid a perfect omelet from the skillet. When she turned around, Bo stood staring at her from just inside the kitchen door. "Are you going to sit down and eat or just stare at me all morning long?"

"What did you do?" he asked.

"What are you talking about?" She set his plate on the table and began filling his mug with coffee as if serving him a fat-laden breakfast were perfectly normal.

Bo walked over and looked at his favorite meal as if it were sprinkled with poison. "You were praying when I walked in and you made me an omelet and bacon for breakfast."

"So?"

"Come on, Judy. I've had nothing but oatmeal and cold cereal for three months. What gives?"

Judy sighed and brought his coffee to the table. "Oh, sit down. I'm not going to snatch it away."

"Are you going to tell me what you've done?" He looked at his plate with a wicked smile on his face. "Or what you want me to do?"

"Why can't I give thanks to the Lord and make your favorite breakfast without you getting all suspicious?"

"Because I know you." He took a generous bite and closed his eyes. "Oh, how I've missed bacon."

She let him enjoy the meal and felt a stab of unease about her motives. His health was more important than the cute smile that graced his handsome face. "Bo?" Judy asked in a sweet voice while rubbing his arm with her hand.

"I knew it," he said.

"What?"

"Just spit it out so I can enjoy my breakfast."

"Fine. I need a favor."

"Must be a big one if I get bacon." He wiped his mouth with a napkin and looked her in the eye. "What is it?"

"I need you to talk to Devon, explain something to him for me."

"Explain what? Quit talking in riddles and get to the point."

"I need you to tell him about a tiny little white lie I told his brother."

Bo set down his fork. "I already don't like the sound of this, and I don't have the foggiest idea what you're talking about."

"I told Phil that Devon had heard some rumors about him, and I need you tell Devon so that if Phil says anything to him, he'll know what he's talking about."

Bo scowled at her. "What kind of rumors?"

She took a sip of coffee and then fiddled with the clasp on earring. "I told Phil that Devon heard he might be gay."

Bo choked on a swallow of coffee. "You did what?"

"Now listen," she said. "I can explain."

"No wonder you were praying. Why would you do that?"

"He's thirty-one years old and he's never brought a woman home."

"You think he's gay?"

"Of course I don't think he's gay, but it was the best I could come up with."

"What do you get out of telling Phil that Devon thinks he's gay?"

"I didn't tell Phil that Devon thinks he's gay; I told Phil that Devon's heard rumors he's gay."

"Oh, well, that makes all the difference."

"Look, Mr. Smarty Pants, it worked. He's bringing a woman home."

"You lied to our son so he'd bring a woman home?"

"Yes. He left me no choice."

"I don't even know how to respond to that." He looked down at his plate and poked the omelet with his fork. "Damn it, now you've ruined my appetite."

"So will you?"

"Will I what?"

"Talk to Devon?"

Bo gnawed on a piece of bacon as if it were a piece of wood. "Why should I? You're the one who lied."

"True, but you're the one who goes by his shop every Wednesday on your way to the Burger Barn."

"I…" Bo averted his eyes. "How did you know about that?"

"This is a small town, Bo. Good Lord, did you really think I didn't know?"

"I was hoping." He sighed and glared at his wife with pity. "Why would you do this, Judy?"

"The boy was a walking hormone in high school. He used to bring girls home from college."

"Mostly to make Julianne jealous," Bo said.

"I know that, but he hasn't mentioned having a woman in his life or brought one home the entire time he's been in South Carolina." She wrapped her hands around the mug. "I'm worried about him, Bo. He needs someone in his life."

"So who's he bringing and what the heck are we going to do with her?"

"I don't know who he's bringing, but I have a few ideas about what to do."

"Uh oh."

"That's part of the reason I was praying. We're going to expand our definition of acceptable behavior in the house for the weekend and I'm going to need you and Devon to move a few things around."

"You need an awful lot from Devon. Seems like you should be the one to explain this plan to him."

"It'll sound crazy coming from me."

"It won't sound crazy coming from me?"

"It'll sound like an order, which it is. Come on, Bo. Eat your breakfast. We've got work to do."

*** 

Margot wolfed down a peanut butter and jelly sandwich at her desk and hoped she'd get at least another fifteen minutes of study time in before Phil returned and she had to quit. She tried to push the afternoon ahead to the back of her mind and zone in on possible arterial blood gas results for a patient with a nasogastric tube attached to low suction. As she figured the levels in her head, the door opened and Danny strode inside the office with Phil in his wake.

"I thought you liked her?" Danny asked Phil over his shoulder as he picked up the message slips she'd left for him on the counter.

Danny had deposited a trail of mud on the new rug and Margot watched Phil's eyes bug out as he knelt down to pick through the thin pile for chunks of dried dirt. "This rug was almost a thousand dollars," Phil said through gritted teeth. "Can't you use the boot scrape by the front door?"

After a cursory glance, Danny shrugged and continued flipping through his messages. "I told you not to spend that much on a rug."

"And I told you that first impressions count, which is why we had to replace the rug we had before." He stood up and looked down at Danny with disgust on his face.

Somehow Phil's scowl and the added four inches didn't faze the builder of their operation. "Sue me," Danny said and continued along the hallway past Margot's desk and into his office. Phil tossed the dried mud into Margot's trash and set a small to-go container on the counter. "I got you carrot cake from

Avenue 12. I know it's your favorite. Would you mind running the vacuum over that, please, before the stain sets?"

Margot shoved her study guide into her oversized bag and wiped the crumbs off her lap. "No problem, Phil, and thanks for the cake."

She pulled the cordless vacuum from her desk drawer and, in three swipes, had what was left of the mess cleaned up. After replacing the vacuum in her drawer, she picked up the thread of the conversation her bosses had started before coming into the office. Danny was laughing.

"A billboard?" Danny managed through strangled breaths. "Where?"

"Along the main road between Echo and Andover. I'm sure everyone has seen it by the way people stared at her at lunch."

Margot fumed at her desk. Kelly Bristow? Was Phil really clueless enough to date trashy Kelly Bristow, the 'Lowcountry's Low Price Leader in Real Estate?'

"I knew she wasn't your type," Danny said. "If this real estate gig hadn't worked out, she'd have been posing for one of those billboards along the interstate promising triple X lunch buffets."

Ha. At least Danny had some sense. Of course, he was from Echo and had probably heard about her less than upstanding reputation in high school.

"Now you tell me."

"Does she know you broke up with her because of the billboard?"

Phil sighed so loud Margot could hear it from her desk fifteen feet away. "Probably, but I don't care. What the heck was she thinking? This is as scandalous as that judge a few years back who admitted he'd fathered a love child with his mistress."

Margot sucked in a breath. Why, of all things for him to compare finding Kelly on a billboard to, why that?

Phil cursed and Margot heard him padding back and forth through Danny's cramped office. "Now I'm really in a bind."

"You should ease up on the women for awhile. Take some time to yourself and play golf or get one of your girly manicures."

"One time I got a manicure," Phil said. "And it was a gift. I told my mom I was bringing someone home for my dad's retirement party. Now I've got no one to ask."

"Sounds like a blessing to me. Those family deals are tough enough without dragging a woman along."

"Yeah," Phil said, sarcasm dripping from his lips. "Must be hard to drag your ball and chain to family functions."

"I'm not talking about Kate."

"Hey, wait a minute." The excitement in Phil's voice had Margot inching down the hallway. "I could take Kate to meet my parents."

"My Kate? Are you smoking crack?"

"I'd just borrow her for a few days," Phil explained. "Nobody would be the wiser."

"If you seriously think I'd let you borrow my wife for a weekend, you've lost your mind. Besides, I'd like to see you explain away the baby."

"Nobody would have to know about the baby."

Danny chortled. "You haven't seen her lately. She's grown."

"She's showing already?"

"She's seven months pregnant. According to her, it's way past time." Danny pulled a file out from under a pile on his desk. "Why did you tell your mom you'd bring someone home?"

"I…" He wasn't ready to tell Danny the reason and listen to the original macho man make fun of his girly ways. "She's putting the pressure on big time for a wife and kids. I thought I'd dangle a girlfriend in front of her to shut her up for awhile."

"Dangling a living, breathing woman in her face won't do anything but fan the flames." He opened the file and began flipping through pages. "I don't know why we're talking about this. Find someone else. I've got work to do."

"Find someone else," Phil grumbled as he exited Danny's office and headed for his own. "Easy for you to say."

Margot scooted back to her desk and patted her fingers along the sleek surface with disgust. Phil had been planning to invite Kelly Bristow to meet his parents! My God, the man was losing touch with reality. She shouldn't care; she shouldn't feel like he'd shoved a knife right through her tender, open, bleeding heart. If Phil Williams could be duped by Echo High's most notorious slut, then she'd wasted years of her life pining after a man with not one brain cell in his head.

She stood up and straightened the neckline of her polyester blouse. Now seemed as good a time as any to announce her resignation. Certainly, Phil would be too upset over losing Kelly to care one way or another that his receptionist, the one woman in his life he could count on, was leaving for bigger and better. She felt a small pang of guilt for kicking him while he was down, but she shoved it aside as she repeated her new mantra. "My new life is just beginning," she said under her breath as she made her way down the hallway toward his office.

She smothered a scream as he bolted out of his door and nearly plowed her over in his hurry to leave. "Phil?" she asked his retreating back.

"I'm taking off early today," he said, lobbing the rubber ball that kept his fidgety hands busy back into his office. "I'll see you in the morning."

"But..." she started, but didn't finish her protest. "I needed to quit today," she said to the door after he'd closed it in her face. Darn it, this was supposed to be the phase of her life where doors were opening, not slamming shut. She turned around and thought about resigning to Danny, but changed her mind when she heard him threatening a supplier that he'd look elsewhere for materials if they couldn't deliver them on time. She'd never intended to speak to Danny about her plans to leave. He was hardly ever around and Phil was the one who ran the office.

Darn it, her carefully laid plans to work her two week notice, take one week for intensive study for the NCLEX, and begin her job after passing the test were going up in smoke. She had half a mind to follow him to the driving range to quit, but she figured she'd never get past the security guard at the country club. Looked like she'd have to wait another day to start her new life.

# CHAPTER 3

Phil couldn't settle his mind on work any more than he could settle his hands as they tapped on the steering wheel along with the beat of George Strait. He'd switched from jazz to country when he needed the familiar sounds of home to help him think. Who could he take to Illinois to meet his parents? He never should have told his mom he'd bring a woman home. His kneejerk reaction to having to defend his sexuality had him backing himself into a corner.

He knew he defined the term metro-sexual—and he hated that term. Yes, he loved clothes, he liked his hair styled, was known for his impeccable grooming, and had a borderline obsession with wine. So what? He was also a rabid basketball fan, a devoted runner, and he started his day with ESPN like every other red-blooded American male. He couldn't stand the thought of his parents or anyone in his hometown thinking he was gay. So instead of taking it like a man and letting it roll off his shoulders, he'd hung himself out to dry by announcing he'd bring a date. Now if he showed up without one, which was highly likely, he'd look like a closet gay who couldn't face the truth.

Jesus, anyone who knew him knew he loved women. He loved everything about them. He loved them so much he'd never been able to settle for just one when so many were out there for the taking. Kelly had been a misstep—a big one. Her charm, her high dollar wardrobe, and her drive to succeed as a businesswoman had lulled him into thinking she was a woman of style. He'd been enjoying her company until she'd plastered her face along the highway like some ambulance chasing attorney out for a quick buck. In Phil's mind, there was a very distinct line between networking and embarrassing pleas for business.

He put Kelly out of his mind as he pulled into his driveway at the Flannery & Williams premier development, Interlude, and hopped out of the car. The place still smelled new, Phil thought as he opened the door and took the stairs two at a time toward his second floor master suite. Of course, why shouldn't it smell new? He was hardly ever home and the lack of furnishings made it seem as if he'd just moved in, as opposed to having lived there for over a year.

He carefully placed his custom-made work shirt into the dry cleaning bin and selected a sage green golf shirt with the Andover logo to accompany his khaki golf pants. He caught himself smiling as he reached for the designer belt he'd splurged on and then grumbled, "Doesn't mean I'm gay. I like nice stuff." He fastened the belt closed and walked out of the closet. "Damn it, now I'm talking to myself."

He brooded on the short drive to Andover and felt only slightly better as the guard waved him through and an eager attendant pulled his clubs from the trunk of his Mercedes.

"You playing eighteen today, Mr. Williams?" he asked. "Got a beautiful afternoon ahead."

"Just the driving range for me, Kyle." He needed a partner for golf and for the weekend at home.

\*\*\*

When Kate Flannery walked into the office late in the afternoon, Margot was reminded of the first time she'd seen the stunning brunette. She'd come to interview Phil and Danny for *Design & Build* magazine and Phil had melted like butter on a hot biscuit when he'd gotten a look at her. Margot felt nauseous watching the scene unfold before her eyes until Danny came into sight, and Kate's color had drained from her face when he walked by without looking up. That's when Margot knew Phil didn't have a prayer with the beautiful journalist who, unbeknownst to all, had

had a prior relationship with Danny. And now, just over two years later, they were happily married and expecting a baby.

"Hi, Margot," Kate said as she turned to close the door.

Margot got a full glimpse of her protruding belly and smiled. "You're one of those annoying pregnant women."

Kate rubbed her mound like a proud mama. "Excuse me?"

"I mean, you're annoyingly skinny. It looks like you've shoved a basketball under your shirt."

"I'm eating like a horse and this is all I have to show for it. But I'm not complaining. At least I'm showing. For awhile there I thought I never would."

"You look wonderful," Margot said.

"I feel wonderful." Kate placed some shopping bags on the couch in the waiting area and eased into the sea grass chair. "I love being pregnant. Oh, God," she said and sat up straighter in the chair. "I am annoying."

"No, you're not. You're just happy."

Kate pushed herself up and waddled over to Kate's desk. "You don't look happy. What's going on?"

Margot sighed. Despite her continued pangs of jealousy for the woman who had it all, Margot had developed quite a liking for Kate. She'd talked to Kate about her plans before, but never with a timetable attached. "I came in today all psyched to quit, and Phil left for the afternoon before I got a chance to do it. I just want to get it over with."

"You're quitting already?"

"I'm done with my coursework. I've got one more test to pass—the big one—and I'm as good as hired at the hospital."

"Margot, that's fantastic. I didn't know you were so close to being done."

"It feels like it's been forever. I'm excited, but change is hard." She looked around the small waiting area. The warm chocolate walls and contemporary furniture provided a stark contrast to the industrial white of the hospital. "I'm ready to take the next step, but I have to quit first."

"Does Danny know?" Kate asked.

Margot felt her cheeks heat. "No. I wanted to tell Phil first since he's always around. I doubt Danny will care one way or the other."

"I wouldn't say that, Margot. He's said more than once he's glad you're around to keep the office in shape and Phil in line."

Margot snorted. "I don't know about either of those things. Phil doesn't even know I exist." Whoops, she hadn't meant to say that out loud.

Kate placed her hand over Margot's on the counter. "No luck there?"

Fear and embarrassment swelled in Margot's stomach as she jerked her hand away and straightened the papers on her desk. "I don't know what you're talking about."

"Yes, you do," Kate said.

It was the pity Margot saw in her eyes that kept her defenses in place. "Phil's my boss. All I meant was that any warm body who can answer the phone, do a little computer graphics, and run some errands would fit the bill around here."

"Okay, if you want to deny what I've seen on your face every time I've been in this office, you can. Believe me, I understand the need to protect your heart."

"Kate, really…"

"I'm done being annoying. I've embarrassed you, and I'm sorry." She straightened and placed a hand on her lower back. "I came by to see if Danny can come to my appointment with me. Is he in?"

Margot shook her head. "He just left."

"Shoot. I tried calling and it went straight to voicemail, which meant he was on the phone. I figured I'd take a shot."

"Are you feeling okay?" Margot asked.

"Yeah, for the most part. I get tired easily and my back is really starting to ache."

Hummm. Constant back pain could indicate pre-term labor, but Margot thought it better not to stress the already anxious Kate. Besides, she was headed to the doctor. "Be sure to mention your symptoms to the doctor."

"Symptoms? Do you think something's wrong?"

"No," Margot quickly backtracked. "But some people think telling the doctor how they feel is complaining. Doctors need to know exactly what the patient is experiencing in order to get a clear picture for diagnosis."

"Spoken like a nurse," Kate said with a smile. She grabbed her bags and went out with a wave.

Margot sat back in her chair and stared at the pencil sketches of completed Flannery & Williams projects along the wall. If Kate knew how Margot felt about Phil, everyone else probably knew also. Oh, God. Maybe Phil knew, too!

She let her head slam onto the desk's surface and vowed to quit first thing in the morning.

\*\*\*

Phil ordered a draft beer after his impossibly bad round of golf. He'd considered it fortuitous to find Dr. Randall McBain on the driving range and in need of a partner. Unfortunately, there was nothing fortuitous about losing fifty bucks and your pride in one fell swoop.

"Drowning your sorrows?" McBain asked with impish grin on his ruddy face. The young doctor couldn't help but rub salt in Phil's wound.

"Just putting a cap on a crappy day." He set the frosty mug on a coaster and faced his regular Sunday golfing buddy. "I'd offer to buy you a drink, but you took all my money."

McBain settled at the bar next to Phil. "Good thing all you need is your signature." He motioned for the barkeep. "I'll have your special on draft." He turned to face Phil. "So what happened today? Break some pencils? Color outside the lines?"

McBain was infamous for his holier than thou attitude. No one's work was more important than his, certainly not an architect's. Even the architect designing the building for his medical practice. "Fuck off, McBain."

"Ouch, Phil. That hurts." McBain laughed at his warped sense of humor. "Seriously, did you kill someone on the table today?"

"Did you?"

"Only if by killing you mean performing my most impressive breast augmentation." He looked down at his outstretched fingers. "These hands are responsible for molding the now perfect figure of the world's hottest college professor."

Phil popped a peanut in his mouth and then nearly choked as recognition hit. "Priscilla Prescott?"

"You know I can't divulge patient information."

The wicked gleam in his eye told Phil he'd hit the mark. "Danny used to date her."

Randall sneered. "I'm glad he's off the market. He really skewed the odds for the rest of us."

Phil couldn't get past the idea of Priscilla having surgery. "I thought her tits were real?"

"My patient's tits," Randall gave an exaggerated wink, "were real. She wanted a lift and my reputation had made its way to her hallowed halls. I should get some sort of academic award."

Phil shook his head. "Is there anyone left on the island you haven't nipped or tucked?"

"Quite a few, actually." He nodded to the bartender when he delivered his beer. "Business should be brisk for the next decade or so."

"I like them real," Phil said before he thought better of getting into a conversation with Dr. Shallow about the merits of real vs. implants.

"I appreciate the appeal of a natural rack," Randall admitted. "At least on the young ones."

"I'd assumed you go for high and tight."

Randall shrugged and took a swig of beer, letting out a comical "Ahhhh" as it slid down his throat. "Nothing better than a cold beer after robbing you blind on the course." He chomped on a handful of peanuts and pondered Phil's question. "I've begun what I like to call a scientific case study."

"Is that so?" Phil asked. He recognized the sarcasm of Randall's response.

"I consider it research. Women want natural looking implants and there's no better way to give them what they want than by...sampling the best of what nature provided."

"I'm constantly amazed at the lengths you're willing to go to for your craft."

"Hey," Randall said with a hearty smack on Phil's shoulder. "Somebody's gotta do it."

"And where do you find these natural beauties?"

"The hospital, my dear boy, is chock full of young nurses. I've got my eye on one very tasty morsel right now."

"The hospital doesn't frown on doctor-nurse relationships?"

"The hospital doesn't know about my relationships." Randall looked appraisingly at the two women who sat next to him at the bar. "Besides, Maggie's not at the hospital yet."

"Still in high school?" Phil asked.

"Just done with nursing school. She'll be on staff in a few weeks, assuming she passes her qualifying exam."

"Well then," Phil raised his glass in toast, "here's to Maggie passing her exam."

"Here, here," Randall said with a devilish gleam in his eye.

Poor Maggie didn't know what she was in for.

# CHAPTER 4

Phil sat staring out the window of his office while absently tossing his ball from hand to hand. His crappy night hadn't gotten any better after two beers and dinner with Dr. Randy. His morning run hadn't done much to cheer his mood one bit. Phil spent most of the night wondering how the egomaniacal doctor managed to lure young nurses into research when Phil couldn't even come up with one woman to take home to meet his parents.

Any woman he'd ever dated before was off the table. He wasn't with them any more for a reason and he wasn't about to cross back over a bridge once he'd moved to the other side. He couldn't take a stranger or someone he'd known for only a little while because that would just be weird. The perfect solution was a woman friend—someone he could explain his reasons to who wouldn't think he wanted more out of them than a weekend of pretense. The problem was he didn't have any women friends.

"Hey," Danny popped his head inside Phil's door and cocked his head toward the reception area. "Where's Margot?"

"She made a run to the shopping warehouse for supplies. Her voicemail said she'd be in around ten."

Danny seemed appeased, but instead of going back to his office, he stood in the doorway and studied Phil. "What the hell is wrong with you?"

"What do you mean?" Phil asked. Danny wasn't one for office gossip and he sure as hell didn't linger in doorways when he could be on the phone or at a building site.

"You look like shit." He made motions toward his head. "Your hair is all messed up and you've got a puppy dog look on your face."

Phil carefully finger combed his hair into place. "I've got less than three weeks to find a woman to ask home with me and I don't have a clue who it'll be."

"Somebody from the country club?" Danny suggested.

"I was there last night. That well is dry."

"Why don't you go into Charleston and hit a club?"

"I'd rather hit myself over the head. Have you been to a club lately?" Phil chuckled at his own question. "Of course you haven't. You're happily married. Clubs make me feel like an old man in a sea of teenagers."

Danny moved to sit in a chair in front of Phil's desk when he heard Margot enter the office with bags in hand.

"What's the big deal anyway? Just don't take someone."

If only he could explain without sounding like an ass. The thought of people thinking he was gay really bothered him. God knew Danny would think it was hysterical. "I have to take someone. I told my mom I would and now I have to."

"Why don't you take Margot?" Danny asked in a weird stage whisper.

"Margot?" Phil choked. "Our receptionist, Margot?"

"Do you know another Margot?"

"I can't believe you, of all people, would suggest such a thing. If I ask her to go home with me for the weekend and pretend to be my girlfriend, that smacks of sexual harassment."

"She's quitting."

"Who's quitting?" Phil asked. Couldn't Danny concentrate on one thing at a time?

"Margot's quitting. If she doesn't work here, she can't accuse you of sexual harassment."

"Why the hell is she quitting?"

"She finished her nursing degree. She's getting a real job."

"This is a real job. Damn it." He pounded his fist on the desk. What else could go wrong? "How do you know she's quitting? You're never in the office."

"She told Kate," Danny said. "Kate told me."

"Why would she tell Kate?"

"They're friends. Sort of. Which is perfectly fine by me since Kate could use some women friends."

Kate and Margot were friends and Margot was a nurse. Phil almost got up to look in the mirror to make sure he wasn't dreaming. "Nursing? Why didn't I know about this?"

"Good question, since you spend most of your day together."

"I thought she was reading romance novels."

"To be honest, I did, too, before Kate told me about her plans." Danny shook his head in disgust. "We should probably start paying more attention to our employees." He stood up and looked down at Phil with his hands on his hips. "So ask her."

"Who?"

"Margot. Ask Margot to go home with you and pretend to be your girlfriend."

Phil sat back in his seat and let his ball slip from his fingers. "Are you out of your mind? She's too young."

"She's old enough to be a nurse."

"Yeah, but she's so...plain. Between her clothes, that snorting laugh of hers, and those crazy curls, no one in their right mind would believe we were a couple."

"Believe it or not, "Danny said, "she might be your only choice."

\*\*\*

Margot stood frozen in the hallway with bags of toilet paper, paper towels, and cleaning supplies fisted in her ironclad grip. She looked down at the skirt she'd bought in high school and the clearance top she'd bought a few years ago. So what if she didn't have even a spare dime to spend on clothes? Pretty soon all she'd have to wear were scrubs anyway. She couldn't help the way she laughed, could she? God knew her hair was out of control, but she didn't have time to straighten it every morning and she certainly couldn't afford a salon treatment for hundreds of dollars. As if to mock her, a blonde lock fell unceremoniously over her eye. She supposed the steam coming from her ears had caused it to fall free of the clips she'd used to hold back her mane that morning.

How dare he describe her like that! How dare he give voice to all of her shortcomings! When she saw Danny's face as he exited Phil's office, she knew he thought she'd overheard their conversation.

"Good morning," he said with a sheepish smile before slinking past her and closing his office door.

"Not for me, it isn't," she mumbled and continued to the linen closet by the bathroom. She set the bags on the gleaming hardwood floor and began slamming supplies onto the shelves. Hearing Phil describe her in those terms certainly eased her guilt over quitting. And to think she'd turned down drinks with a doctor in order to study and work up the nerve to let Phil down easy. She crumpled the plastic bags in her fist, shoved them in the recycling bag she'd installed in the office, and marched to the entrance of Phil's door.

She took a deep breath and gave the trim a hearty rap.

Phil's head swung around as the sound of her knocking echoed off the walls of his office. "Margot. You're back."

She swallowed hard, took two steps inside, and announced without preamble, "I quit."

The sight of his jaw going slack and his inability to form words should have been comical from the man who always knew just what to say in any situation. "Huh?"

Unrequited love turned quickly to unworthy injustice in a finger snap. "I believe you heard me," she said with her chin in the air.

"Margot…"

"I'll give you two weeks and not a second more."

Phil unfolded himself from his chair and stood to look down at her. She wouldn't be swayed by his impressive build or the weary look in his warm, candy colored eyes. "I understand you're studying to become a nurse?"

"Studying is over…almost over. One more test and I'll be on staff at the hospital."

"I know I should offer my congratulations," Phil said. "But I can't seem to feel anything other than sorry you won't be around."

Sorry my ass, she screamed inside her head. What a relief for him not to face her unsuitable clothes, her unsightly hair, and unbecoming laugh every moment of the day. "I'm sure you won't have any trouble finding a more appropriate replacement."

He lifted his brows, blinked hard once, and lowered his eyes to the desk. "I hope you don't think—"

"Don't worry, Phil. I don't think anything at all. Would you like me to place an ad in the paper or would you?"

He shot her an insipid glance. "Why don't you write something up and let me take a look at it first?"

"No problem," she said and turned to leave.

"Margot?" Phil called.

She turned around slowly, afraid the indignation she'd felt earlier would burst free in a jagged sob from her aching throat. "Yes?"

He seemed to study her in the doorway, his eyes sweeping from her bargain shoes, over her seasons-ago-fashionable skirt, to her hand-me-down blouse. "We'll miss you around here."

Ha. "You won't even know I'm gone."

# CHAPTER 5

Phil slammed his Mercedes into park when he saw Danny's truck backing out of their lot. He shot to his feet and jogged to the driver's side window before his elusive partner snuck away. Phil flagged him down just as Danny had removed the phone from his ear and had turned his tires toward the exit.

"Did you get a chance to look over those resumes I put on your desk?" Phil asked after Danny lowered the window.

"I haven't had time," Danny said. "I'm playing catch up on the Millhaven project thanks to the permit issues. I'm barely treading water."

Phil sighed in frustration. "I'm not hiring a receptionist without your approval."

"Just pick one, Phil. I trust you." Danny tapped his fingers on the steering wheel as beads of sweat formed along his brow despite the cooler October temperatures. Danny wiped his forehead with the sleeve of his t-shirt.

Phil noted Danny's red face and neck and was tempted to suggest he use sunscreen, but Phil knew better than to offer advice when Danny was in a mood. He'd been in a mood for over a week now. "Kate still not sleeping?"

Danny jerked the truck into park and blew out a breath as he drew his hands through his hair. "Her back still bothers her at night, so she can't get comfortable." He rapped the steering wheel with his fist. "Damn it, Phil. What kind of parent am I going to be if I can't stand the sight of my wife in pain? How the hell am I going to make it through delivery?"

Phil lifted his hands in surrender. "You've just stepped way outside my area of expertise." Phil resisted the urge to shudder. "From what I've seen in the movies, you just hold her hand and tell her to breathe."

"She says all I need to do is make sure she gets an epidural."

"Epidural?" Phil asked.

"Pain meds."

"Ahh." Phil felt a stab of loss for Danny's bachelor days. Their morning conversations used to be a lot more interesting and, for Phil, much more relevant. What was next, breast-feeding? "So let me run in and grab the resumes. You can take them with you, look over them at lunch or whenever you get a second."

"I'm not going to have a second," Danny said. He put the truck in drive as way of ending the conversation. "And I seriously don't care."

"Just narrowing them down to ten took me forever," Phil complained. "Now they're just names on a page."

"So," Danny said as he reached for his phone where it had begun to ring, "call them in for interviews."

"Ten interviews? I don't have time for that."

Danny pointed to his phone. "I've got to get this." He eased off the brake and brought to the phone to his ear. "Have Margot interview them first," he said before pulling away.

Hummm. Why hadn't he thought of that? Margot knew the job inside and out. She'd be able to narrow the choices and possibly pick her successor. If only he hadn't blown it with her and blurted out those comments about her hair and clothes.

He'd worked hard over the years to establish a good rapport with her and, in one moment of panic, he'd ruined it. Now, instead of her happy smile, she greeted him with an eye roll and a scowl. He never knew how much he'd looked forward to her good-natured cheer until it was gone.

Determined to win her over, he retrieved his suit jacket and breakfast from the car and started up the stairs to the small house they'd converted to their home base seven years ago. He loved the porch they'd added and the decorative door with beveled glass he'd designed and Danny had made to order. He spied the plants wilting in the urn. He'd have to replace the vinca he'd planted with pansies as soon as the cooler weather decided to stick.

They'd contracted a designer on the interior, but he'd known what he wanted from the beginning. Warm browns on the walls, softer beiges in the fabrics and rugs. Everything about the house invited people to come in and stay for a while. He'd framed his sketches of their most impressive projects for the walls and had even had a few offers for commissioned drawings.

He opened the door expecting to find Margot behind her desk, but all he found was her bag on the counter. He set the blueberry scone he'd bought for her at the bakery on a napkin and continued down the hall. She came out of the bathroom and glared at him in greeting. Great, he'd have to spend another day sucking up.

He didn't like how ever since she'd tendered her notice she'd dropped all pretense of civility. He knew she'd overheard his nasty comments. He hadn't meant to say those things so loudly and certainly hadn't meant to hurt her feelings, especially since he was just desperate enough to ask her to spend the weekend in Cash with him.

She'd started wearing more casual clothes, he'd noted with interest. Gone were the ugly polyester shirts and paper-thin skirts with ratty hems. Today she paired a snug graphic t-shirt with cargo pants. Her attire, while completely inappropriate for the office, emphasized a nice rack he hadn't noticed before, but also underscored her age. She looked like a teenager.

"Good morning," he said with exaggerated cheer. "I brought you a scone."

"Thanks," she said and continued past him to her desk.

He watched her scoop up the scone and napkin and drop them in the trash. He reminded himself not to lose his temper, and it helped when she blushed knowing he'd seen her throw his gift away. "I was wondering if you'd mind setting up interviews with the ten people left on our list. I'd like for you to do the initial interviews and narrow my choices down to two or three.

You know what we need, and then I'll decide from the ones you think will work best."

"Fine." She sat down and started typing on the computer. "Your mother called this morning." She handed him a pink message slip without looking up. "Something about flight details."

He grabbed the sheet and crumpled it in his fist. He hadn't forgotten he only had two days before the rates went sky-high.

***

"So what's it like to work for them?" Sonja D. Frank, current cashier at a warehouse store and one of the ten applicants for her job, asked during an interview.

Margot gave her the standard answer she'd come up with after being asked the question four times previously by different applicants. "They're fine as long as you do your job and are respectful to clients." Margot let her eyes drift to the hallway where she knew Phil was huddled over his desk working on the designs for a new medical practice. She thought back over the last three years as Sonja went on about her previous responsibilities as head cashier. If Margot were honest with the applicants, she would have described Danny as occasionally grumpy, incredibly focused, and out of the office as much as possible. Whenever he worked in the office, he was either on the phone or working up bids with his door closed, and she knew not to disturb him. Kate was the absolute light of his life and the thought of becoming a father had him completely freaked.

As for Phil…she sighed wistfully. Phil Williams could talk anyone into just about anything. He was as slick with his tongue as he was with his drawings. Working with him the past three years was like having an apprenticeship in personal negotiations 101. She intended to draw upon his tactics when dealing with patients in the hospital. But he was more than just that silver tongue; he was a man who paid attention. He planted pretty flowers in the urns on the porch and remembered to water them regularly. He always brought her little treats during the day—

28

breakfast from the bakery, dessert from his lunches out, cards and gifts on her birthday and secretary's day.

She'd been intentionally rude to him in the last week, and as she escorted Sonja out of the building, she felt guilty for that as she spied a cookie on her desk. Damn him. White chocolate macadamia nut—her favorite flavor, and just in time to satisfy her afternoon sugar craving. She picked up the spreadsheet she'd finished and the cookie and took her first bite as she made her way to his office.

Absorbed. That's how he looked at the drafting table with a pencil in his hand, his brows furrowed in concentration, those long limbs jutting out over the desk as he worked out his ideas. Just once, she thought as she watched him from the doorway, just once she'd like to know what it felt like to have Phil look at her the way he looked at his work, serious, loving, totally enthralled.

She must have sighed because his head whipped up and around. She'd broken the spell between the design and its master. "Interview over?" he asked as if coming out of a fog.

"Yep." She took a step inside. "Four down, six to go."

"Anyone satisfy your standards?"

"Not as satisfying as this cookie." She waved the half-eaten treat in the air. "Thank you."

"I'm glad to see it didn't end up in the trash."

She felt her cheeks heat. "Touché."

He swirled around to face his desk after his eyes did a quick scan of her dumpy clothes. She'd had to revert back to her ugly wardrobe for the interviews. "Can we call a truce for the remainder of your time here?"

"I'm not mad at you," she said.

His grin, the sideways lift of his spectacular mouth, had her rooted to the floor. "Liar."

"Well," she dropped her eyes and shuffled her feet. "I'm not mad anymore."

"Good." His grin bloomed into a full glorious smile showing off his perfect teeth and the crinkles around his eyes. "No more casual Tuesdays?"

"I didn't think the casual look would send the right message to your future employee."

He eyed her again, his gaze lingering on her chest. She was used to men staring at her breasts, but not Phil. "I like you in casual clothes. You look more…you, I guess."

Don't, she wanted to say. Don't do this to me again. Don't suck me in just as I'm trying to make a clean break. But because she would never admit her feelings out loud, she said, "I've got the cost report on The Moorings." She set the papers on his desk and turned to leave.

"Margot?" She spun around at the sound of his voice. "I appreciate you doing the interviews."

"It's no trouble," she lied. It was a huge pain in the butt and had kept her from studying for the NCLEX.

"I'm sure you'll find the right person, but no one can fill your shoes."

"My ugly shoes," she chided.

He ducked his chin and she felt sure if she were standing within reach, he would have patted her head like a child. "Your practical and highly efficient shoes."

She tried to smile before returning to her desk. At least she knew how she'd be remembered: practical, efficient, and utterly boring.

# CHAPTER 6

Phil had to do it. He had to make plane reservations by midnight and he was down to only one option. And damn Danny for shoving her in his face so that all others paled in comparison.

He'd racked his brain for someone to ask. He'd gone to the country club every day for lunch or dinner or drinks. Nothing. He'd gone to Charleston and club hopped twice and left both times with numbers in his pocket for women he'd never call. He'd even gone so far as to invite an old girlfriend to lunch. She'd walked in sporting a three-karat diamond on her left ring finger and he knew he was screwed.

When he called Margot into his office and asked her to shut the door, he mentally appraised his soon to be ex-receptionist. He had to admit she had a nice build. She was shorter than the women he usually dated, but nicely proportioned with an impressive chest he wasn't sure how he'd managed to overlook for the past three years. She wore understated makeup that never managed to hide the smattering of freckles across her gumdrop nose.

It was the hair, he could admit after his quick, but honest review, that made her look like she'd just hopped out of an hour long ride in a convertible. Her frizzy blonde curls seemed incapable of taming, no matter what clip or contraption she tried to force them into. They hid her most alluring feature, another thing he'd only recently discovered: her wide-set, fawn colored eyes. Her perfectly shaped brown brows made him wonder what color hair she had in other parts of her body.

He gave himself a mental shake as she took a seat in the chair facing his desk. This was Margot, for Christ's sake.

She crossed her ankles and linked her fingers, a look of suspicion on her face. "What can I do for you?"

"That's…the perfect opening to this somewhat awkward conversation," he said. In a tactical move he'd perfected early on in his career, he came around the desk and sat next to her in his other guest chair. "Margot, I've got a rather large favor to ask of you."

She tucked a stray lock of hair behind her ear where it immediately sprang back into her eyes. She blew it away with a breath. "I'm not willing to work beyond our agreed upon termination date. I've got a lot of studying to do and with these interviews—"

"I don't need you to work past next week, but…" He found himself fidgeting in his seat as her eyes narrowed with suspicion. "I do need a favor. Not a boss-to-employee favor, but a friend-to-friend favor."

She seemed ready to bolt from the chair. Her chest heaved up and down and her lips twitched into a grimace. "You want me to be your pretend girlfriend?" she spewed as if he'd implied he wanted her to strip naked and perform a lap dance.

"Well, yes." He ran an unsteady hand through·his hair and stood up to pace. "I've got to go home for my dad's retirement party and I can't go alone."

"Why not?"

"I just can't. Since I quit seeing Kelly, I don't have anyone else to ask."

Margot stood up and stepped into his path, stopping him mid-stride and forcing him to meet her stare. "You want me to hop on a plane to Illinois and pretend to be your girlfriend and you won't even tell me why?" She let out an insipid snort. "I don't think so."

When she turned to leave, he reached out and lightly grabbed her arm. "Margot, please, hear me out."

"Are you going to tell me why?" she asked.

"Are you going to make me?"

She crossed her arms over her chest and gave a snorting snicker.

"Fine!" He raised his hands in surrender and tossed himself back in his desk chair, forcing her to sit across from him yet again. His mouth had gone bone dry. "Some people in my hometown think…there's some gossip going around about me…" He hung his head in shame and blurted out the truth without looking her in the eye. "I need people there to know I like women."

In the silent seconds that followed, he held his breath before lifting his head to gauge her reaction to his most embarrassing admission.

"People think you're gay?" she asked. The way she gaped at him in stunned surprise made him feel worlds better.

He gave a cheerless laugh. "Can you believe it?"

She regarded him for a second and then shrugged. "Kind of."

"What?"

"I mean, if I didn't have first hand knowledge of your speed dating, I might assume the same."

"Why?" he asked. "And what do you mean speed dating?"

"Oh, come on." She sat up, ready to argue. "You bounce from girl to girl faster than cue balls on a pool table."

"That's insulting and completely untrue."

She lifted those mocking brows. "I call them like I see them."

"Sounds like you need glasses." He leaned back in his chair and they stared at one another across his desk like a couple of kids on the playground. "So, if you didn't know any better, why would you think I'm gay?"

She raised a shoulder in tandem with the blush creeping up her neck. "You're always so…groomed."

"Groomed? Good grooming means I'm gay?" He dismissed her with a wave of his hand. "Please."

"And color coordinated."

He gloried in the hole she dug for herself. He'd never heard such ridiculous excuses. "Yes, matching outfits screams homosexual."

"I'm not finished," she chided. "You garden and you know the names of colors beyond the basic color wheel."

"I'm an architect."

"Exactly." She raised her finger in the air. "Not an interior designer."

"This proves nothing. Any man on the street knows colors."

She fixed him with a smug smile. "If Danny were in the office, I'd prove you wrong in a heartbeat."

"How so?"

"I'll name three colors. If you can describe them," she twitched her lips, "you're as good as gay."

"Bring it on, sister." He rubbed his hands together and waited. Surely he wouldn't know her choices. By the way she narrowed her eyes in thought, he knew she'd give him a zinger.

"Bisque," she offered.

"That's not even hard," he rolled his eyes. "And it's a popular wall color. Light beige."

"Okay," she said as she roamed the ceiling for more challenging colors. "Periwinkle."

"Light purple, but everyone knows that." He splayed his hands on the desk. "Give me a hard one or this test is obsolete."

He took in a deep breath and he felt his heart beating faster. This little game had turned ugly and he didn't like it one bit.

"Puce."

Phil inhaled sharply. He knew puce, of course he knew puce. Kind of like putty, mostly like puke, a dull, purplish brown. Damn it.

"Ah ha!" she wailed, pointing at his face. "I knew it." She reached for the phone. "Call Danny and prove me right."

"This doesn't prove anything!" He slapped her hand away and shot to his feet. She did the same. "You only gave me one hard one and Danny is hardly a good barometer." He slapped his hands on his hips. "How do you know puce?"

"It's the color of the scrubs at the hospital. Nobody looks good in puce."

"This is stupid," he shouted. "I'm not gay!"

"Are you homophobic?" she asked.

"No," he answered quickly, a little too quick judging by the way she frowned at him.

"You are homophobic. But why? You know you're not gay, I know you're not gay, and pretty much every living, breathing thing on the island knows you're not gay. So what's the big deal if some yahoos from home think you're a dandy?"

He slunk back into his seat and wanted to ignore her question. He wanted to snatch back his asking her to go with him and erase the whole afternoon. But because he couldn't and because she stood there staring down at him as if he'd lost his mind, he had to answer. "My dad is the original macho man. He's never understood me or my career or my life. So instead of trying to understand or just accept that we're different, he's the kind who makes fun." He lifted his eyes to find her listening raptly. "I've been called more gay slang than you probably even know."

"Well, that's…" she sat down in the chair and reached her hand out to rest it atop his, "just plain awful of him."

"I will admit to intentionally grooming well whenever he's around just to piss him off."

"Can't say that I blame you."

"Margot," he settled his hand over hers and sandwiched her pale fingers between his, "if people are talking about me back home, he's either furious that I'm making an ass of him or too embarrassed to show his face. Either way, if I show up alone…" He sat back in his seat, let out a defeated breath, and hoped beyond hope he'd convinced her to help him out.

"I, I don't know, Phil." She pulled her hand away and rubbed her crinkled brow. "I've set aside next week for intensive study and you said yourself no one would believe we were together."

He grimaced. "You really heard that entire conversation?"

"Enough to make me mad."

"I'm sorry," he said. He'd obviously hurt her feelings and yet she still looked ready to give in to his request. "I never would have said those things if I thought you'd hear."

"I know that," she said. "You're never intentionally mean."

"You think I'm mean?" he asked. No one had ever described him as mean.

"Insensitive, yes, and occasionally self-absorbed, but not mean."

"Oh, well, that makes me feel worlds better." His attempt at sarcasm didn't even make her smile.

"I'm going to have to think about this."

"Okay, but I should probably tell you that I need to book the flight by tonight."

"Tonight?" she squealed. "You need an answer by tonight?"

"Not until almost midnight."

"Oh, well. That make me feel worlds better," she mimicked his Midwestern drawl to perfection.

"Please, Margot, just think about it. It's only a weekend. The party's on Saturday night and we'd be out of there early Sunday. You could study on the plane and God knows there's nothing to do in Cash."

"Give me some time to think, Phil. If you keep trying to sell me on the trip, I'm going to get mad and turn you down flat."

"Okay," he stood up and walked her to the door. "I'll be right here whenever you decide."

"Yeah," she said. "I know where to find you."

***

Margot parked at the end of the long drive and looked up at the impressive structure. Two stories of sand colored, rammed earth with an intricate garret's nest at the top. She imagined the view over the trees facing the ocean was perfect for watching the sunset and wondered what it felt like to be blissfully in love and have the perfect house for romantic nights.

As if she'd conjured her, Kate appeared on the doorstep, rubbing her back and holding a large black and white dog by its collar. Margot got out of her car and joined them on the porch.

"I see you found it okay," Kate said.

"You gave perfect directions." Margot leaned down and tapped the dog on its head. "Your home is beautiful, Kate."

"Thanks." She led Margot past the foyer and into a two-story den featuring a massive stone fireplace. "Go to bed, Teddy," Kate ordered and pointed to a large crate in the corner of the room. The dog obediently jogged to the crate and laid down on the dark cushion embroidered with his name. "Danny built this place from scratch. Every time I walk in, it's like getting a great big hug."

"There you go being annoyingly happy again," Margot said.

"Sorry. Jeez, no wonder I don't have any friends."

Margot gaped at Kate as she sank into the leather couch. "You don't have any friends?"

"I didn't mean to say that out loud." She maneuvered a small pillow behind her back and let out an audible sigh. "Danny's been harping at me to make girlfriends, but I haven't exactly meshed with the ladies on the island. I'm hoping once the baby's born, I'll find a group of new moms."

"The ladies on the island fall into two basic categories," Margot explained and sat in an oversized fabric chair. She felt swallowed up as it drew her against the fluffy back and left her feet to dangle. "The new residents tend to hang around the country club and shops around Andover. The natives, like me, stick to Echo. You're kind of an in-betweener being married to a native, but not native yourself. Besides, I've heard more than one woman complain about you snatching Danny off the market."

"Believe it or not, I've heard that myself," Kate complained. "One woman actually told me not to get too comfortable in his life because he'd dump me within a month. When I explained we were married, she nearly swallowed her tongue."

"Oh," Margot laughed. "I would have loved to have been a fly on the wall."

"As satisfying as it was to set her straight, I think the encounter only added to my reputation. So," she readjusted the pillow and stretched her legs out on the couch, "what's the big emergency?"

Margot dropped her face into her hands. "It's Phil."

"What's he done?"

"He asked me to go home with him."

"What?" Kate dropped her feet to the floor. "How…when…?"

"Not home with him as in to bed with him. He asked me to go home to Illinois with him for the weekend of his dad's retirement party."

"Oh. Okay." Kate's brow furrowed over her electric blue eyes. "I'm confused."

"So am I." Margot shot to her feet and began pacing in front of the fireplace. The dog lifted his head, but stayed put. "He needs me to go with him." She stopped and held her hand up to Kate like a traffic cop signaling to a driver. "Correction, he needs someone to go with him and he's so desperate he asked me."

"Why does he desperately need someone to go home with him? As far as I know, he's never taken a woman home before."

"That's the problem, and before you ask me what that means, I'd better tell you I can't explain."

"Okay…"

Margot continued along her path, back and forth in front of the imposing glass coffee table topped with books and a beautiful pottery bowl filled with river rock. "So he's desperate and he's asked me and he needs an answer by tonight."

"Tonight? When did he ask?"

Margot looked at her watch. "About thirty minutes ago."

Kate shook her head in dismay. "For a man who appears to have it all figured out, he certainly takes a wrong turn every now and again."

"What should I do? I mean, I know I shouldn't go—it's ridiculous to even consider going, but he's so good at making me feel sorry for him. He practically admitted he scoured both islands and Charleston proper for a more suitable woman and yet I'm seriously considering going." She halted and faced Kate. "What is wrong with me?"

"For starters, please sit down. You're making me dizzy."

Margot curled up in the chair and tucked her legs under her. "Sorry."

"Now, nothing is wrong with you except that you've got a serious crush on him and have for some time."

38

"True," Margot admitted. Amazing how an hour ago she would have denied it, but now, with Kate, she found it easy to face her most shameful secret. "Which makes the fact that I'm considering going that much more stupid. I've got a lot at risk. This crush, for lack of a better term, could morph into something more dangerous if I spend the weekend with him. On the other hand," she said before Kate could interject, "it could prove why we'd never make a good match. This whole experiment could finally break the spell I've been under and help me make a clean break." She took a deep breath and looked at Kate. The perplexed expression on her face made Margot feel a little light headed and queasy.

"Sounds like you've made up your mind," Kate said.

"No, I'm of two minds, and I'd like for you to help me choose which one to go with."

"Why don't you ask yourself how you would feel if you turned him down?"

"Well," Margot dropped her knees and imagined walking into Phil's office to decline his offer of help. "I'd probably feel guilty and selfish."

"Why?"

"Because he's got a pretty good reason for needing someone to go home with him. I'd much rather it be me than his usual dating disaster."

"And how would you feel if you accepted?"

Margot dropped her eyes and played with the fraying edges of her skirt. "I'd feel nauseous and a tiny bit excited," she admitted. "I'd also feel like I was setting myself up for heartache."

Kate sat back against the couch and sighed. "You want to know what I think?" When Margot nodded her head, she continued. "I think if you didn't go, you'd be giving up an opportunity to find out what could have been between the two of you."

"Don't misunderstand, Kate. He's not asking me because he's in any way interested. He told Danny I was young and plain. *'Between her clothes, snorting laugh, and crazy curls, no one would believe we were a couple.'*"

"Well, you do a mean Phil impression. And I do mean mean."

"He didn't know I was listening."

"I'm sure that didn't ease the sting," Kate said.

Margot couldn't stand the pity in her eyes. "It helped me to quit and it certainly helps me understand exactly what he's asking for with this trip. I've got no illusions about his intentions."

"So with no illusions or expectations, are you going to go?" Kate asked.

"I came here hoping you'd talk me out of accepting, but you haven't done that."

"Sometimes you have to take a risk. There's no guarantee it'll work out, but you'll never know if you don't try." Kate looked down at her hands where she twisted them in her lap. "If he breaks your heart, are you going to blame me?"

Look at her, Margot thought. The woman with everything didn't have everything after all. "I could use a friend as much as you, Kate. If things don't work out, I'll do the mature thing and blame Phil."

"Good." Kate eased up from the couch and reached her hand out for Margot. The dog got up, stretched, and wagged his tail. "Come with me and we'll see what we can do about your clothes."

# CHAPTER 7

Phil sat in his office and tried to work the design for the restaurant they were building on Andover, a project he'd fought hard to win and one that deserved his full attention. But he couldn't concentrate on anything but what was going on in their lobby. The girl Margot had recommended and he'd hired had the loudest voice. As he sat back in his chair, reached for his ball, and began tossing it from hand to hand, he decided loud wasn't the most appropriate word. Annoying. There was something about her voice that grated on his nerves.

He'd have to learn to live with it, he told himself and flicked the ball away, stood up, and closed his office door. He returned to the computer and his initial drawings, but he still couldn't concentrate. He felt silly for feeling panicky at the thought of Margot leaving. She was their receptionist, not a major player in their organization. She'd made it sound like a monkey could do her job the way she went on about how much time she'd had to study over the years. But something about the change in employees had him feeling uneasy.

He considered the fact that maybe he felt edgy because, in one day, he and Margot were scheduled to leave for their weekend in Cash. He'd been thrilled when she accepted and had spent the last week sharing detailed notes on his family history and what to expect when they arrived. She'd rolled her eyes every time he'd handed her another typewritten sheet and tucked it away in her bag. He only hoped she'd read his mini-biographies of his brother and his wife, his mom and dad, and the assortment of people they were certain to run into over the weekend.

He called, "Come in," to the knock on his door and felt relieved to find Margot alone on the other side. "Good," he said. "Come on in and sit down. I need to talk to you."

She stayed at the entrance of his office, her hand still on the doorknob. "I just wanted to let you know that Rebecca and I are going to the office supply store."

"Oh," he said. "I guess we can do this when you get back."

"I'm leaving on time tonight, Phil, so whatever you want is either going to have to wait or you can give it to Rebecca."

"I need to talk to you about the trip." He pulled more notes from his briefcase and caught the tail end of her look toward heaven. "I've typed up a few more notes and I'd like to go over them with you."

"It'll have to wait until tomorrow," she said.

"We leave tomorrow." He sighed and looked down at his calendar. He'd scheduled a haircut for later that night and had to run by the dry cleaner and pack, but if she was going to be difficult… "I guess we can do this over dinner. I'll have to reschedule some things, but why don't you meet me at that new café on 5th around 6:30?"

Margot's cheeks turned a delightful shade of pink before she shifted her glance to his floor and said, "I can't do dinner tonight. I have a date."

"A date?" He couldn't have been more surprised if she'd said she was running with the bulls. "You're going on a date the night before our weekend together?"

"You mean our 'pretend' weekend together? Yes, I'm going on a date."

"Well…"

"Look," she said. "Our flight doesn't leave until three. We can either go over your notes in the morning or on the plane." She stepped back. "Don't worry. I'm a quick study."

When she shut the door in his face, he felt…angry and a little bit upset. They were supposed to be in sync with each other for the weekend. How was that supposed to happen when she would be full of whomever she planned to spend the evening with?

And just who the hell did she plan to spend the evening with?

\*\*\*

Margot tried to ease the tension that had settled just at the base of her skull without drawing attention to her rising headache. She didn't want to be distracted while dining at a restaurant she'd wanted to visit since she'd heard Phil rave about its inventive Italian dishes. She didn't want to be irritated that her date seemed perfectly fine with the snail's pace with which the meal was progressing. She didn't want to wonder if Phil was jealous she had a date. She didn't want to think of Phil at all.

Phil was her gold standard, the man she judged every other man against, and even though his shine had dulled in the last few weeks, she felt more excited than she should to be spending the weekend with him and his family. That excitement and her mental list of things to do before she left had the muscles of her neck seizing just as dinner finally arrived.

"You're really tense tonight, Maggie," Randall said before popping a bite of Parmesan encrusted salmon in his mouth and letting out a moan of delight at its flavor. "I'd be happy to use my magic fingers on you later."

She just bet he would. Dr. Randy, as the nurses liked to call him, had a reputation as the cockiest surgeon on staff at Charleston General. He, like everyone else at the hospital, called her Maggie after her nurse instructor refused to listen every time she'd tried to correct the shortened version of her given name, Margaret. She'd skirted Randall's invitation for weeks and had finally given in just to remind herself of what was left in the dating world if she crashed and burned on her weekend with Phil.

"I'm going out of town this weekend, so I've got a lot on my mind."

He topped off her very excellent glass of cabernet. "You must not be worried about the NCLEX."

"I plan to study this weekend and all the following week. I'll pass," she said with an affirmative nod of her head. She'd worked too hard for too long to get this close and blow it at the end.

"I'm looking forward to seeing you at the hospital," Randall said with a decidedly wicked gleam in his eye and a toast with his glass.

Dr. Randall McBain had reason to be cocky. He'd made a name for himself as a plastic surgeon at a very young age. His volunteer work with children with facial deformities had caused her to accept his offer of a night out, despite the fact that it was the last thing she wanted to do. "So tell me about your trip to Brazil," she asked.

"It was exhausting, as all the missions I've been on can be, but Rio is such a beautiful country." He slathered butter on one of the restaurant's famed garlic rolls and continued while chomping on the bread. "The beaches are magnificent and the food is incredibly fresh."

Margot swallowed her spicy pasta dish and had to take a drink of water to cool her mouth. "I'm sure Rio is gorgeous, but I meant the surgeries. How many kids with facial deformities were you able to help?"

"Oh," he dabbed at his mouth with the napkin. "Probably close to a hundred. You wouldn't believe some of the living conditions these kids face. It was…" He took a sip of wine and Margot almost sighed as she anticipated his description of heartbreaking sadness. "Disgusting. I don't know how people live like that."

She dropped her fork and began rubbing her neck with both hands as her muscles tensed. Good Lord, if he kept talking, she'd end up in a neck brace.

"Hey, you okay?" he asked with genuine concern.

She nodded and tried to placate him with a smile. He'd gone on mission trips with the Sunbeam Foundation for several years and changed countless lives for the better. Cut him a break, she told herself and offered up another question. Surely he wasn't as shallow as he sounded. "How many countries have you visited?"

"Six so far, and Brazil's definitely my favorite. I try to stick to Mexico and South America. They've got some Middle Eastern trips and some to China, but I figure, why go so far from home? Besides, I've had enough patients from India to know I couldn't stomach the smell for a week."

"Randall, that's a pretty blanket statement for an entire region of the world."

"Hey," he said with a calculated twitch of his lips, "if the blanket fits."

After a painfully long dessert where she kept the conversation clear of politics, religion, or anything that might tempt her to throw her fork in his eye, he walked her to her car where she'd parked along the curb.

"Thanks for dinner, Randall."

"The evening doesn't have to end with dinner." He reached around and began using those magic fingers on her neck. "Wow, you're tight as a drum."

It took several seconds for Margot to respond. He really did have a knack with those hands. "I'm headed out of town tomorrow, remember?"

"Where are you going?" he asked as he circled her neck and used his thumbs at the top of her spine.

"The Midwest." She felt grateful her words had come out of her mouth as a squeak instead of a moan.

"Why in the world?" he asked. "I think I'd prefer India."

He'd loosened her up enough to laugh. "A favor for a friend."

He maneuvered around to face her, his hands cupping her face. "Must be a good friend. It's just as well. My sister's in town for the weekend."

Before she knew how it happened, his lips were on hers, lightly, lingering, just enticing enough to make her forget they were along a pedestrian street and that she really didn't like him. Like him or not, the man could kiss and it had been a long time since she'd been kissed. He pulled back before she had to insist and flashed a smug smile.

"That ought to hold us both until you get back." He plucked the keys from her hand, unlocked the door, and ushered her inside.

She nodded like a robot and started the car. He waved her off as she pulled onto the street. Had she agreed to see him again? Damn it. Maybe there really was magic in Dr. Randy's hands.

# CHAPTER 8

"What happened to you?" Phil asked as he stepped inside Margot's house and stared at his receptionist. Except she didn't look like the same person who'd strolled out of his office that morning. Gone were the flyaway curls and dumpy clothes. Before him, in the tidy little den of her house, stood a flaxen haired beauty. Her curls had been tamed into silky waves that landed just above her breasts. Her teal wrap dress showcased every curve and angle of her petite little body.

"What happened to you?" she asked with a puzzled look on her stunning face. He couldn't decide what surprised him the most, the glossy thickness of her hair, her athletic, hourglass figure, or how he tingled when her yellowish brown eyes made quick work of his attire.

"It's the corn belt, Margot, not Fifth Avenue. What did you think I'd be wearing?"

"Um," she said and tapped a polished finger against her chin. "Not designer jeans, cowboy boots, and a flannel top. Where'd you buy that getup? The local feed and seed?"

"What about you?" he asked. "Since when do you wear silk wrap dresses and peep-toe sling backs?"

"Since you called me plain. Kate took mercy on me and let me borrow some clothes."

"I hope you packed some jeans and t-shirts, because we're not going to the country club."

She slung a very nice leather hobo bag over her shoulder and reached for the handle of her suitcase. "Of course I packed jeans. What am I? A moron?"

At the moment, he'd have to say she was a very sexy, very irritated woman. And he felt like he'd stumbled into an ambush. He'd felt uneasy as he'd pulled up in front of her cottage home after she'd barely spoken three words to him at work except to shout her address when he'd insisted upon picking her up. She'd been awfully pissy at work for a woman who'd been wined, dined, and kissed silly on the sidewalk of one of Andover's busiest streets. He'd never felt more stupefied than when he'd stepped out of the takeout place and seen her in a lip-lock with Dr. Feelgood. He wrestled the handle of the suitcase out of her grip and held the door open for her.

"I can get it myself," she said as she locked the two deadbolts.

"Crime bad in this area?" he asked.

She breezed past him on the narrow walk and wobbled to the car like a runway model on her first trip down the catwalk. "My mother was a bit of a safety freak."

"This is your mom's house?" He knocked her hand away and opened the passenger door for her.

She sighed and angled herself into his Mercedes. "It used to be."

After tossing her suitcase in the trunk, he joined her in the car. The enclosed space only amplified her scent, something floral and fruity and erotic as hell. Damn it, the weekend was off to a difficult start.

For a week, he'd imaged the weekend in his head and detailed the playbook he'd drawn for Margot to study of his history and his family. Now, only four-hours from game time, she decided to go rogue. "I wasn't expecting you to be so...to look so..."

"So what?" she asked with a deliberate flutter of her mile long lashes. She'd even hidden her freckles behind a layer of foundation.

"So sophisticated. I kind of gave my mom the impression you were young and earthy."

"I thought your family wouldn't buy you dating someone young and earthy?" she threw back in his face.

He let out an exasperated sigh. "Did you bug my office?" He looked over at her in his black leather seats. The dress had parted over her crossed knee and exposed a distracting amount of leg. He motioned for her to cover herself up. "That's why I gave them a heads up."

"Dressed like this, they might buy the fact that we're together," she explained. "I'm young and earthy, yet sophisticated and fashionable." She sneered at him and spoke in a sugary sweet voice. "We're perfect for each other."

"Did you read the new bios?"

She sighed. "Yes, Double-Oh-Seven. You can quiz me on the plane."

"That's not necessary. If you say you know it, then I believe you."

"Good," she said.

"Now that I've been to your house," he said as an intro to something that had bothered him the moment he'd pulled up in front of her mailbox. "I realize I don't know anything about you."

"We've worked together for three years, Phil."

"Yes, and yet I didn't know the job was just a stepping stone for you on your way to bigger and better."

"Only because you didn't ask or pay any attention."

That had certainly been true. Of course, if she'd worn that dress, those heels, and the sexy perfume to the office, he probably would have noticed. And that didn't speak very highly of him. "So give it to me now. You're living in your mom's house. Where is she?"

She turned to look out the window. "She died when I was eighteen."

"Oh," he said. Just because he couldn't see her face didn't mean he couldn't hear the sadness in her voice. "I'm sorry to hear that. It must have been hard."

"It was."

"Any brothers or sisters?"

49

She swallowed hard and twisted her hands in her lap. "Nope," she said. "Just me." She swung her head around and plastered on a smile that didn't quite reach those fetching eyes. "So, your brother Devon sells farm equipment and breeds horses?"

"I thought you read the bios?"

"I did. I'm just trying to make conversation."

"Yes," he said through gritted teeth, and then deliberately relaxed his jaw and shoulders. "Devon's also married to his high school sweetheart and has two perfect children for my mother and father to spoil."

"You're jealous?" she asked.

"Jealous that my younger brother has only been with one woman, has never been farther from home than the Wisconsin Dells, and sells tractors and balers and a hundred other pieces of equipment I can't name? Absolutely not."

"I see," she said, with a nodding of her head that had her waves bouncing like a model in a hair commercial. "You're just a snob."

He leered at her. "You mean a gay snob."

She gave a snorting chuckle that reminded him of who was underneath the polished exterior. "Yeah, lest I forget."

He pulled into a parking spot at Charleston International Airport, turned the car off, and looked Margot in the eye. "Ready?" he asked.

"Ready or not." She took a deep breath that had her chest rising provocatively. "Cash, Illinois, here we come."

***

Margot kept sneaking glances at Phil during the bumpy flight. He looked ridiculous in a plaid flannel shirt so new she was surprised she didn't see a tag dangling from his sleeve. He couldn't have been more obvious if he'd donned a Halloween costume. As she fidgeted to adjust the pushup bra Kate had insisted she wear with the dress, she knew they both felt uncomfortable and wondered for the millionth time what in the world had possessed her to accompany him on this farce.

"So," Phil said as he settled into his seat after a trip to the bathroom. He'd combed his hair, Margot noted as he clicked his belt in place and pulled it tight across his waist. "How was your date?"

"It was fine." She looked up from her study notes to find him staring at her with a stony expression on his face.

"Where'd you go?" he asked.

"Di Paolo."

"Um, very nice. I took Kelly there a few weeks ago. Did you have their tiramisu? You'd love it."

"No, I had pie." She flopped her papers in her lap and went on impulse. "So why did you and Kelly break up?"

He sighed and looked up at the ceiling of the plane. "She was a bit flashy for my taste."

"She was all about the flash. She always has been."

"I guess I mistook her flash for…sophistication. I can't stand to date a woman with baggage."

"Baggage?"

"The billboard ad. Scandalous, to me, equals too much baggage."

So noted, Margot thought. She couldn't think of another woman, Kelly included, who had more baggage than she did.

Phil gave her the once over. "I guess your date didn't keep you out too late?"

"Nope," she said and drew her eyes back to the sample questions she'd printed off the Internet.

The signs and symptoms of an abdominal aortic aneurysm couldn't keep her attention as she felt his gaze on the side of her face. She'd tried hard to put her date in the back of her mind. It hadn't been hard with all the packing she'd had to do to get ready for the trip. She hadn't let herself wonder why she felt so ambiguous about Dr. Randall McBain. He was certainly a step up from her last boyfriend, the auto parts cashier whose only goal in life was to record an album with his garage band. Why she'd wasted even an ounce of her time on someone so completely void of ambition had her grappling with an ugly truth. She was lonely.

As soon as her mother had died, she'd thrown herself into nursing school and work at Flannery & Williams. Her single-minded determination to pay her bills and better her life had left her little time to do anything other than grieve and study. With the finish line in sight, she felt strangely apprehensive about swapping her day job for a career, and the only reason she could come up with as to why was that she'd have precious few people with whom to celebrate her success. Her date with the reputed ladies man of Charleston General had left her feeling more alone than ever.

Phil tried to tuck his long legs under the seat in front of him as the flight attendants pushed the drink cart past their aisle. He bumped her legs in the process and leaned over her shoulder.

"What are you studying?"

"Sample questions for the NCLEX," she answered without looking up. She could tell he was bored and becoming more restless by the minute. She reached her hand out to still his bobbing leg. "Do you have to pee again?"

"No. Sorry." He drummed his fingers on the armrest and looked around the plane. "When I was little, we'd always drive to our vacations. My brother and I used to play this game where we'd look out for other cars and try to guess where they were going by the style of car and the people inside."

"That's very inventive."

"It used to drive my father crazy," he said, "but my mom would end up laughing and joining in eventually."

"You sound just like the Griswolds."

He bumped her shoulder with his. "I figured you were too young to know the Griswolds."

So much for studying on the plane. She sighed and tucked the pencil behind her ear. "My mother was a huge Chevy Chase fan. I've seen all the Vacation movies."

"Perfect," he said. "If you're a Chevy Chase fan, this game should be right up your alley."

"I said my mother was a Chevy Chase fan."

"What kind of movies do you like?" he asked, flipping open the clasp to his watch and shutting it over and over and over again. He was having a harder time sitting still than the little boy in the row in front of them.

"I like those silly horror flicks where the girls are too stupid to live and there's plenty of blood," she said.

"Yuck."

She gave a snorting laugh when he cringed. She kept forgetting to use the giggle she'd practiced instead of her unfeminine snort.

"I suppose you prefer a good chick-flick?" she asked.

"Very funny. I like a legal thriller or a suspenseful action movie, as the heterosexual macho man that I am." He deepened his voice and bunched his arm into a muscle.

She felt her resolve melting as the brilliance of his smile and eternal energy radiated off him in waves. He wrestled the notes from her fist and held them out of reach. "Come on, Margot. You're ignoring me."

"I'm studying, which is what you promised I'd have plenty of time to do."

"You've got all weekend and next week to study. Besides, there's no movie, I forgot to bring something to read, and you're sitting there like a bump on a log."

"I'm studying," she said and made an ill-fated reach for her notes. His arms were so much longer than hers she may as well have been reaching for the sun. "Fine, if you're going to be a juvenile, we'll play."

"Okay," he said and rubbed his hands together like a mad scientist. He looked past her toward the man sleeping on Margot's left with his head against the open window. "We'll start with him," he whispered in her ear. "What do you think?"

She couldn't think at all with his breath on her neck and the familiar scent of his woodsy cologne distracting her senses. She glanced over and made quick note of the gentleman's pinstriped button down, the briefcase tucked under the seat in front of him, and the large college class ring on his right hand.

"He works for a computer start-up," she whispered back toward Phil. "He's leveraged everything he's got to cover his mounting gambling debts and is on his way to a meeting with a potential client that could save his ass." She studied the man's chubby face, slack from sleep. "He was up all night practicing his presentation and his wife's pissed he never came to bed."

"He's not wearing a ring," Phil pointed out. "Why do you think he's married?"

"He's too macho to wear a ring and it really cuts down on his chances to score a quickie while he's away from the nagging wife and the kids."

"Kids?"

"Two," she said. "Boy and girl. They got married when she got pregnant."

"Interesting. So his career's on the line and he's still up for some out of town nookie."

Margot shrugged. "Men are pigs." She was enjoying their repartee, the feel of his arm pressed against her side, and way his eyes laughed into hers a little too much. She straightened in the seat and cleared her throat. "Okay, your turn." She scanned the aisles for their next victim. "Him, over there on the right, two aisles up. The one with the fedora and the sunglasses."

"Well," he said with a delighted grin. "He's a record producer."

"On his way to St. Louis?" she asked.

"Let me finish. There's an Internet sensation, a ten-year-old girl, prematurely developed with the golden pipes of Lady Gaga."

"At ten?"

"I'm going to tape your mouth shut," he said and wagged a finger in her face. She was tempted to bite the end. "As I was saying, she's become famous, and he's on his way to bid for her affections and for her signature on the contract he's taped to his chest. See," he pointed when the man looked over his shoulder and gazed around the plane. "He's nervous because there may be others on board trying to get to her first. The hat and glasses are just a disguise."

"A very poor one, if you ask me," she said.

"Which he didn't." Phil glanced about the plane and nodded with his head at the flight attendant. "What about her?"

"The flight attendant?"

"Sure," he said. "She looks a little too old to be working the aisles. I think there's a story there."

Margot laughed. Their fun came to an end as the attendant in question served them drinks and a tiny bag of peanuts. "What do you think people think when they see us?" she asked.

"Us? Hummm." He rubbed his chin and narrowed his eyes. "Well, you look like a young newscaster on her way to cover the big strike at the dog food factory in St. Louis. You're scared and excited and just hungry enough to make the story worth watching."

It didn't escape her notice that he'd called her young again. Just when she thought they'd made some progress. Although why she thought the fact that he'd asked her to play a game he used to play as a child meant anything other than he thought of her as a kid was simply wishful thinking. She was going to get hurt this weekend because the more time she spent with him, the more relaxed they became with each other, the more her attraction deepened. Knowing the only thing he felt for her was a fleeting sense of gratitude only seemed to make matters worse.

"Why the frown?" He drew his finger along the line between her brows. "I thought we were having fun?"

"You didn't say what people thought of you," she reminded him. If he kept staring at her with his eyes wide, she was tempted to do something stupid and profess her love or burst into tears.

"Nope," he said. "You have to do me."

She'd do him, all right. In a hot New York second. So, to protect her heart, she decided to be mean. "You're plainly an equipment salesman who breeds horses on the side. Your father is about to retire and you're worried he's going to interfere with your business, so you've thrown your older and much more attractive brother under the bus by starting rumors that he's gay in order to shame him home and run interference."

His mouth puckered in annoyance. "That wasn't in the profile."

"I read between the lines."

# CHAPTER 9

Cash hadn't changed. Main Street windows were decorated with paint for the Cash High School Cougar's football game and people sported the familiar blue and yellow attire. As he and Margot drove through downtown in their rental sedan, he felt excited to see his mother as they approached his boyhood home. The closer they got, the more Margot squirmed in the seat next to him. She'd already chewed off her lip gloss during the hour drive from the airport and stared nervously out the window.

"Are we almost there?" she asked for the millionth time.

"Just another mile or two. Traffic is starting to jam up because of the game."

"What game?"

He spared her a glance at the ridiculousness of her question. "It's Friday. High school football? Cheering crowds? Horny teenagers? Adults reliving their childhood? Any of this sound familiar to you?"

"Oh." She shrugged. "I guess."

"Don't tell me you weren't a loyal Echo Egrets fan?" He signaled for a turn past the grocery store where he'd worked as a clerk in high school.

"Not so much."

"Why not?" he asked. He couldn't imagine not going to support the home team. "What the heck did you do on Friday nights in high school?"

She stared at her lap for a moment before raising her eyes to his. "My mom was in the hospital a lot. Going to games didn't seem that important at the time."

He didn't miss the edge in her voice that told him to back off that particular subject. It was just as well. He didn't know what to say and they'd arrived at his drive.

"This is it?" she asked as he pulled the car to a stop in front of the rambling old farmhouse. He wondered why his parents had never gotten a smaller house that didn't require so much upkeep after he and his brother left the nest. His dad had put a fresh coat of brick red paint on the door and shutters and the setting sun shone brightly off the polished windows. He hoped his parents hadn't gone to any trouble for his visit home with Margot. Knowing his mom, she probably had.

"Home sweet home." He hopped out, stretched his back, and was on his way around the car to open Margot's door when she opened it herself. For a moment, his mouth went dry as she swung her legs to the ground and gracefully climbed out of the car.

He didn't like the path his male addled brain had decided to take with Margot, zooming straight from a semi-friendship to noticing the curve of her backside and her slender, tapered ankles. He felt very grateful she'd worn those boxy clothes to work all these years or else he would have had a hard time keeping his eyes and his hands to himself. He started to look away when he realized his appreciation for her would go a long way toward convincing his parents she was his girlfriend. He closed the door for her and thrust her against his chest, locking his arms around her tiny waist. She felt like a doll in his arms.

"What the hell are you doing?" she asked with an irritated line between her brows.

"We're dating, remember." He dipped his head and nuzzled her neck. He got a whiff of her perfume and almost took a bite out of her delicate skin. "If you don't act like you like it, my parents are going to get very suspicious."

As if on cue, his mother stepped onto the porch and let the door slam at her back. "Well, well, well. Look what the cat finally dragged back in."

He pulled away from Margot to stare at his mother. The wind whipped her dark hair into her eyes and she'd draped a royal blue sweater over her shoulders. Her jeans were well worn in the knees and her bright pink jogging shoes made him laugh out loud. "You going to the game like that?" he asked.

"You know I don't wear yellow." She walked down the steps and, when she reached the bottom, extended her hands to encase Phil in her long and sturdy arms. She smelled like cinnamon and goodness.

"It's good to see you, Mom."

"It's been too long, Philly." She gave him one last squeeze and shoved her arm through his before turning to look at Margot.

Margot's cheeks turned pink as she extended her hand with a nervous smile. "Mrs. Williams. I'm Margot Manning. It's so nice to meet you."

His mother cradled her hand in hers. "I'm Judy Williams. What a lovely name you have, Margot. Sounds kinda like a movie star, doesn't it, Phil?"

He cocked his head to the side and pondered his mother's question. This new Margot certainly was putting on one hell of a show. The wind tossed her carefully controlled tresses into disarray, helping him snap out of the weird place he'd let himself visit. Margot. Young Margot with the crazy hair and ugly clothes. Except she'd buried her mother and put herself through school. And when she put a little effort into her appearance, she didn't seem so young after all.

"You both must be starving after traveling all afternoon." His mother led them up the stairs and inside the house. "I've got some stew on the stove and fresh bread in the oven. Why don't you grab your bags, Philly, and let Margot freshen up until dinner's ready?"

He heard her talking, he knew she wanted him to get their things from the car and get settled, but he felt overwhelmed by the sights and smells of his home. The familiar squeaking of the screen and the cracking pop it voiced as it slammed shut. The smell of dinner in the kitchen and the slightly musty undercurrent even his mom's best potpourri couldn't mask. The faded braided rug under his feet and the wood in the fireplace waiting to be lit. He felt years older in the house that seemed to have shrunk around him, and yet as young and carefree as the child who'd once claimed it his own.

"Phil?" His mother slapped him on the shoulder. "Go get the girl's bags, honey. She looks ready to drop."

He looked over at Margot. She didn't look ready to drop, she looked anxious and alone, twisting her hands together, her eyes wide with appeal that he snap out of his reverie and throw her a lifeline. "Mom, Margot loves sweet tea. Would you mind getting her a glass while I bring the bags in?"

"Headed that way," his mom said with a wave of her hand. As he stepped onto the porch, he heard his mother compliment Margot on her dress.

He gathered Margot's suitcase and makeup bag, along with his hanging bag and travel case, as quickly as he could. He didn't want to leave his mom and Margot alone for too long without him there to run interference. As much fun as he'd had with Margot on the plane, they should have spent a lot more time syncing their stories. He was half way up the staircase to the second story when he heard his mother call, "I put fresh towels in the guest room, Phillip, and cleaned out some space in the closet. Put your bags in there and then come on down."

The guest room? Surely she meant for him to put Margot's bags in the guest room. He wheeled her suitcase into the room with buttercup walls and the queen sized iron bed. The sheer curtains fluttered in the breeze and his mom had placed a finger vase of daisies on the nightstand. He could envision Margot there, her curls across the soft blue pillowcase, snug under the heavy white quilt his grandmother had made.

He continued to his room on the same floor and stopped dead in his tracks at the threshold. "What the hell?"

He dropped his bags on the wooden hallway bench and jogged down the steps. His mom and Margot sat at the round kitchen table, sipping tea from old Coke glasses. "Mom. Anything you want to tell me about my room?"

She smiled up at him like the Cheshire cat. "You mean my new office? Do you like it?"

"What do you need an office for and why did you have to use my room? What about Devon's?"

"Devon's room is too dark and yours looks out over the meadow. It's a happier view."

"A happier view," he muttered under his breath. "Where's all my stuff? And where do you expect me to sleep? In Devon's room?"

"Your stuff is in the barn. If you'd ever drive here, you could go through it and take what you want so we could get rid of the rest."

"Get rid of it?"

"What is with you and your brother? Really, you should have seen the fit he pitched when we gave his bed to Goodwill."

"When you...what did you put in his room?"

"Your daddy's been exercising. I got him one of those stepping machines with the TV attached and some free weights." She patted Phil's stomach. "He's lost fifteen pounds."

"Really? That's great. I've been hounding him for years to do something about his potbelly."

"It's more like an anthill now," she said with a wink.

He joined them at the table and reached for Margot's glass. She tried to swat his hand away, but he snuck a quick sip first. He could have wept from the taste of his mother's tea when suddenly everything she'd said hit him like a fist to the face. "You gave away Devon's bed?" he asked.

"Yes," his mother said with a disapproving glance. "We needed room for the equipment."

"I know, but...where am I supposed to sleep? On the couch?"

She bolted out of her seat and lifted the lid off the stew steaming on the stove. "The guest room, of course."

He looked at Margot. Her eyes bulged and she fumbled the glass of tea in her grasp. He'd never expected to sleep with her under his parents' roof. He'd made it perfectly clear the sleeping arrangements wouldn't be an issue as his parents would never in a million years let one of their sons sleep with a woman in the same room in their house. He knew it had been a long time since he'd been home, but it sure hadn't been a million years. Margot kicked him under the table.

"Ouch." He leaned down to rub his aching shin. "Mom," he said and stood up to talk to her face-to-face. He couldn't stand Margot's accusing stare. "That's not necessary. I know how you and dad feel about unmarried couples sleeping together under your roof. Neither of us would want to make you uncomfortable."

"Sweetheart," she tapped the spoon on the edge of the pot and reached out to squeeze his arm. "You're thirty-one years old. Seeing as how you've never brought a woman home, your dad and I aren't going to make you two pretend you're not sleeping together. We're fine with it."

"You're fine with it," he repeated. Who was this woman and what had she done with his mother? "That's very considerate of you and dad, but I won't put you or Margot in that position. I'll sleep in the den. It certainly won't be the first time."

His mother turned around and, after giving Margot a forced smile, the same smile he'd seen her give to Mrs. Collinsworth after she'd given his mom a backhanded compliment after her second place finish in Cash's annual chili cook-off, said, "Nonsense. You'll sleep in the guest room with your girlfriend and that's final."

Phil looked at Margot. Her eyes had turned dark with annoyance and her mouth twitched. She looked ready to take a swing at him if he dared step closer. He took a chance when he saw her open her mouth to speak. He yanked her chair back from the table and pulled her to her feet. "I'll just show Margot to her room and let her change for the game." He ignored the sting of her nails biting into his hand. "Kickoff still at seven?"

"Seven sharp," his mother said. "Give me fifteen minutes to get dinner on the table."

"Great." He dragged her from the room and up the stairs. Dinner with his family, a high school football game, and sleeping with his ex-receptionist and pretend girlfriend in his boyhood home. What could be better?

***

Margot was momentarily distracted from her red-hot anger by the sights passing by her. Fireplaces set with wooden logs waiting for a match and an evening at home. Fluttering curtains, worn rugs, rocking chairs, family photographs framed along the creaking staircase. Phil's house screamed HOME as much as the needlepoint pillow she'd noticed on the chair in the foyer announcing they were Home Sweet Home.

He practically shoved her into an upstairs bedroom and leaned against the closed door, staring at her with one brow raised. "I know this isn't what you agreed to," he said with his palms in the air. "I'm not real thrilled about it either."

Of course he wasn't thrilled. She felt sure the last thing he wanted was to sleep in the same bed with her. Other than panic and an upset stomach that could very well be due to the ultra-sweet tea, she wasn't exactly sure how she felt about the turn of events. Phil's mother, Margot could tell, was up to something.

"Your mom planned this, Phil. She's a part of the plan."

"What plan?" he asked. "My mother would never allow us to sleep together under normal circumstances."

"What's so abnormal?" Margot asked. "You told her you were bringing someone to stay for the weekend. If she really had a problem with us sleeping together, she would have made arrangements to have a bed brought in."

"Hummm. You may be right." He paced across the room and pivoted at the base of a beautiful iron bed. The ancient quilt had daisies that matched the flowers in a bud vase on the lone nightstand. "But why would she violate her own moral code? Do you think she really thinks I'm gay?" He slapped his hands on his head and yanked on the ends of his hair. Margot had never seen him so upset or so unconcerned about his locks. "My God. My own mother!"

"I don't know what her motives are, but between the two of us, I'm the one who needs consoling. You said I'd have my own room!"

"I couldn't have anticipated this turn of events, Margot. I swear this is the last thing I expected to happen. My brother and his wife couldn't even sleep in the same room when they were engaged."

"What are we going to do?" she asked. All Margot could think about was the sexy nightgown Kate had insisted she pack "just in case" something happened. She'd look and feel like a fool slipping between the simple cotton sheets in a sheer chemise, and the only other thing she'd packed were her Scooby-Doo sleep pants and matching Shaggy top. In the immortal words of her favorite comic hero, Ruh-Roh!

Phil looked around the sparse room. The only other piece of furniture besides a chest at the end of the bed was a wooden rocking chair in the corner. "I'll sleep on the floor."

"Phil, you can't sleep on the floor. What about your back?"

"What about my back?" he asked. He looked a little wild with his hair mussed and his hands on his hips.

"Your basketball injury? How do you think your back would feel after sleeping on hardwood floors?"

"That was a pulled muscle, like, two years ago." He cocked his head and studied her as she felt a blush creeping up her face. "I can't believe you even remember that."

Whoops. She'd admitted too much and needed to diffuse the situation. "Neither one of us is sleeping on the floor." They both eyed the bed. Margot couldn't even imagine Phil's body fitting between the ornate headboard and low scrolled footboard. Out of sheer necessity, they'd be all over one another. "We'll just have to share."

"Margot." He dropped his hands and moved to stand before her, gently placing his hands on her shoulders. The pitiful look of appeal on his face spoke volumes about his interest in sharing the bed. "You have my word I won't take advantage of the situation. I promise nothing will happen."

"Trust me, Phil. Your disinterest in me is obvious." She pulled out of his grasp and heaved her suitcase onto the open luggage rack in the corner. She unzipped her bag and rifled through her things to gather what she needed to change. With her arms full of clothes, she turned to face him. "Where's the bathroom?"

"Across the hall." She moved past him and had her hand on the knob when he said, "I'm really sorry about this, Margot."

Not as sorry as she was going to be when the weekend was over.

The bathroom door wouldn't lock. Of course. Margot stood looking at her reflection in the mirror and fought back tears. What was she doing here? How was she going to protect her heart when every time Phil opened his mouth, he shot daggers straight into her chest? She took a deep breath and assessed her appearance. The dress had held up well over the very long afternoon. Kate had been right about that, at least. Her hair was another matter. Corkscrews were popping out at the top of her head and after she slipped out of her dress and put on the shirt she picked out to wear to the game, it looked as though she'd reached the end of the frizz control's limits. She ran her fingers through her hair and dabbed at the mascara leaking around the edges of her eyes. It would have to do, she thought as she stepped into the hallway and saw Phil lounging on the bed of their room, waiting for her to return.

She had to fight the urge to drop her things on the floor and fling herself on top of him if only to show him what he could do with his sorry. When he sat bolt upright and turned to face her, she thought he'd caught her staring and could read her mind. "What's wrong?" she asked.

"My father's home."

# CHAPTER 10

Judy Williams gasped when her husband entered the kitchen through the side laundry door. "Oh, Bolton, you scared the life out of me."

Bo set his things on the counter and leaned over her shoulder to sniff the soup she was preparing to ladle into bowls. "I saw a car in the drive. Are they here?"

"Upstairs now. They'll be down any minute."

"What do you think?" he asked.

Judy set the ladle down and turned into her husband's arms. "Oh, Bo. I like her. She's not at all what I expected."

"What do you mean?"

He tried to grab a biscuit from the cookie sheet and she swatted his hand away. The man wouldn't lose any more weight if he kept nibbling between meals. "I mean she's...petite and blonde. She's all dolled up, but there's something wholesome about her underneath. I like the way she looks at Phil."

"You think it's for real?" he asked. "I thought you were worried he'd bring any old woman home."

She tapped her finger to her lips asking him to please keep his voice down. There was no way for them to come down the creaking stairs without notice, but she didn't want to take the chance her husband's deep baritone would carry. "I thought he would if he didn't have someone special in his life, but I get the impression there are feelings involved."

"I'm still not real sure why you did this. Don't you think if he were serious with a woman, he'd eventually bring her around?"

"Bo, I can't wait to meet my future daughter-in-law on the eve of the wedding. He's been down in South Carolina for too long. He never talks about the women in his life and if I have to use underhanded tactics to find out about him, I will. The good Lord knows my motives are pure."

"The Lord may know, Judy, but the citizens of Cash sure don't. I can't stand people thinking he's gay because Devon can't keep his mouth closed."

"Devon told me you're the one who blabbed while a customer was in the store."

Bo tried again to reach for a biscuit and Judy maneuvered between him with a breadbasket. "I was whispering," he said. "He's the one who can't talk without shouting. Paul Reynolds' son overheard and the next thing I know he's screaming, 'Daddy, did you know Mr. Williams' son is gay?' Devon was so embarrassed he made sure Paul knew it was Phil and not him. Now everybody knows."

Judy shook away the unpleasant idea that Phil's reputation had been ruined by her antics and insisted it would all work out in the end. "So Margot solves everyone's problem. He can show her off this weekend, we can find out more about our son's future, and we'll squelch the rumor at the same time."

"I don't know, Judy. I've got a bad feeling about this."

When the stairs began groaning under the weight of their guests, she shushed her husband and waved her arms in the air. "Act natural," she told him. "The show is about to begin."

***

Phil placed his hand at the base of Margot's spine and carefully led her toward the kitchen where he knew his dad was waiting. He didn't remember being this nervous when he'd first brought Julianne home at the tender age of sixteen. Of course, what parent didn't want their son to date the beautiful daughter of the town's most respected minister?

Phil wasn't nervous about convincing them he and Margot were a couple; for the last few hours, he'd had a hard time convincing himself they weren't a couple. When she stormed into the bathroom, he'd walked over and fingered a piece of lace lingerie that had draped over the edge of her suitcase. He reclined on the bed and tried not to envision her wearing the sweet nothing when he heard the roar of his dad's engine outside. Dread crawled up his spine like a spider up a web. Bo Williams had come home to face his pansy son.

Margot stopped dead in her tracks in the middle of the hallway, only inches from the kitchen door. She spun around and looked up at him with panic in her eyes. "I need to go change," she said and slid past him onto the stairs.

He caught up with her when she'd only gotten three steps up, turning her around. For the first time, they stood eye to eye. "Why do you need to change? You look…" He hadn't really noticed what she had on as he'd been so focused on the upcoming confrontation with his father. He glanced down at her cheetah print ankle boots, army green cargo pants, and tight white t-shirt hiding under a denim jacket with a cheetah scarf. She looked like a sexy kitten on the prowl. "You look amazing," he said with a purr in his voice even he recognized as a come on. "Don't change a thing."

"Are you sure?" She sandwiched her bottom lip between her teeth and her eyes glimmered in the muted light. Had he ever noticed the flecks of gold against the brown?

"Margot…" His body moved toward her like a magnet.

The sound of his mother's voice had him pulling back with a jolt. "Dinner's ready," his mother called. "If you two are going to eat before the game, we need to get to it."

"Don't change," he said.

She rewarded him with an unsteady smile and nodded her head. "Okay."

He slid his hand down her arm and laced his fingers through hers. When she didn't move, he gave her a gentle tug and she joined him at the base of the stairs.

He didn't feel nervous walking into the kitchen where his dad poked through the breadbasket while his mom carried bowls to the table she'd set. He felt confused by the woman at his side. He couldn't quite put a name to the feelings she stirred, but he did know they made him uncomfortable. What had he been about to say to her when his mother called them into the kitchen? Had he really considered kissing her? His universe, it seemed, had turned on its axis.

His dad dropped a biscuit on his plate and dusted his hands off on the orange napkin that matched his mother's sunflower themed kitchen. He got to his feet. "Phil," he stuck his hand out, forcing Phil to drop Margot's hand. His dad inspected him from head to toe. "We're going to the game tonight, son, not the rodeo. What the hell are you wearing?"

"Dad," Phil said, ignoring his father's insult. "This is Margot Manning. Margot, my dad, Bo Williams."

His father fumbled around the table and gave Margot a dainty handshake. Phil had never seen him act so clumsy.

"It's nice to meet you, Mr. Williams," Margot said. "You have a beautiful home and I appreciate you welcoming me into it this weekend."

"Oh, we're glad you're here, Margot. And please call me Bo."

"You two have a seat," his mother instructed. She ushered them to the built in bench along the window. His mother and father sat in the chairs opposite Margot and him. "Go on and get your fill. The burgers at the game don't taste nearly as good as they smell. This should tide you over until later. I've got pie in the oven for after the game."

"Apple?" Phil asked hopefully.

"Of course."

"Margot loves pecan, but she's never tasted your apple, Mom." How had he come to know Margot's taste in food, he wondered as he shoveled in spoonfuls of stew. He'd gotten into the habit of bringing her snacks, mostly the sweet kind, not long after she'd first begun working at the office. He'd never given much thought to why he brought her sweet treats or how her simple appreciation of them kept the tradition going. When she really liked something he'd brought her, she'd give a moan of delight. Maybe they'd eat their pie in the bedroom later and see just how—

"Phillip?" His mother asked. "You're a million miles away."

"Sorry," he said. "Is everything set for the party tomorrow?"

"As set as its going to be," his mother said. "I'm going over to the American Legion tomorrow afternoon to decorate with Sheryl."

"Sheryl's my sister-in-law," Phil explained to Margot.

"I know," Margot said without thinking. "She owns the flower shop. She and Devon have been married for eight years."

"Well," his mother's eyes lit up with delight. "I guess Phil does mention us every now and again."

Margot flashed him a playful grin that had the blood draining from his brain. "You'd be surprised how much I know, Mrs. Williams."

"Call me Judy." Phil passed his mom the butter tub after she'd put a biscuit on her plate. "So tell us about you, Margot. What do you do?"

"I'm a nurse, well…almost a nurse. I take my licensing exam next week, and then I'll be on staff at the hospital in Charleston."

"A nurse? How exciting. I can't stand the sight of blood."

"That's fairly common," Margot said.

"And does your family live in the area or are you a transplant like Phil?"

"I was born and raised in Echo. My mother died a few years ago."

"I'm so sorry, dear." His mom reached out and patted Margot's arm. "I lost my mother two years ago. I can't imagine how hard that must have been for you and your father."

"I've never met my father."

"You haven't?" Phil asked before he thought better of revealing how little he knew of her personal life. She spared him a fleeting glance before dropping her eyes and fiddling with her spoon.

"How about you, Judy?" Margot asked. "Do you work outside the home?"

Phil had to stifle a snort. His mother hadn't been employed in over thirty years and if Margot had read his bios she would have known.

"Oh, I haven't had a job in years, not since putting Bo through school. I do some volunteer work for the church and I run a book blogging site."

"A book blogging site?" he asked before Margot could get the words out.

"Honey," she said with a pink glow to her cheeks. "You know how much I love to read. Devon set me up a website and I post reviews and do author interviews. I've got over five hundred followers."

"Followers?"

"For the blog," she answered. "I'm even on Twitter."

"You're on Twitter?" he asked.

"The book blogging community is very forward thinking. I'm on it all—Facebook, Twitter, Google plus. If you'd ever get on Facebook like I asked you to, this wouldn't be a surprise."

He washed away the distaste in his mouth with a swallow of tea. "I hate that kind of stuff, Mom."

"You may hate it, but it would do wonders for your business."

He put his spoon down after finishing the bowl. "Business is fine." He looked at Margot and smiled. "Can you imagine if I asked Danny to get on Facebook?"

"How is Danny?" Judy asked. "Such a surprise to hear he'd gotten married and is now expecting a baby." She glared at her son. "His family must be so proud."

"Shocked is more like it," Phil said. "No one ever thought he'd settle down."

"Amazing what the right woman can do to a man. Isn't that right, Bo?"

"Yeah, yeah," his dad mumbled and then thankfully changed the subject. "So how's business, Philly? You working on anything big?"

His dad thought he should be designing skyscrapers or at least multi-story office buildings. Phil felt sure his dad equated environmentally friendly residential and commercial buildings to gay bars. "We've got another development in the works, but with the economy the way it is, we're scaling back. We should break ground on a doctor's building after the first of the year."

"You are?" Margot asked. "I don't remember you mentioning that. Which practice?"

Oh, this ought to be good. If only they were alone and he could press her for information. "Randall McBain," he said and sent her a pointed stare. "He's a golfing buddy and a plastic surgeon. We discussed his building on the course. Have you heard of him?"

Her brows lifted under her bouncing curls and her eyes darted to the stew. "The plastic surgeon? Yes, I've heard of him," she said.

He should have asked if she'd ever been kissed by the scalpel wielding skirt chaser. All of the sudden it struck him. He was spending the weekend with the possible girlfriend of a friend. He and Randall had played golf together for over two years and, despite their different outlooks on life, they'd developed a friendship of sorts. He wouldn't poach a friend's girlfriend. Furthermore, McBain was a client. Which made Margot completely off limits. Shit.

His mom stood up and carried Bo's and her dishes to the sink. "We'd better get a move on if we're going to make kickoff. Phil," she called over her shoulder, "you and Margot take a separate car in case those bleachers get my hip to acting up. I wouldn't want you two to have to leave early."

He didn't want to go at all, but he'd suggested the game to his mother earlier in the week thinking a public outing at the football game with his "girlfriend" in tow would squelch the gay rumors fast. Now the only thing he wanted to squelch was his mounting desire for Margot.

# CHAPTER 11

Margot felt nervous as Phil inched the rental into a parking lot in a grassy field across from the football stadium. The Cash water tower loomed over the distant trees illuminated by the football lights.

"We don't have to stay long," he said.

"It's your weekend," she said and reached for the door handle. The feel of his hand on her sleeve had her turning around to face him.

"Margot, I'm sorry this weekend hasn't started out so well. I know you're uncomfortable sleeping in the same room, and I promise you'll have time to study tomorrow."

"Look, Phil, its fine. We're here to clear up your reputation. If we have to sleep in the same room to do it, that's okay. It's not a big deal." She couldn't sit there another minute in the small space with a console and a mountain of lies between them. Sleeping with him was the biggest deal in her life. She opened the door, careful not to hit the car next to them, and took a gulp of fresh air. She could smell the grass under her feet, the rich pungent soil of the Midwest, and felt as if she'd landed on another planet. There were no ocean waves crashing just beyond the line of trees, but miles of freshly plowed farmland. She felt adrift in the waving plains of wheat or whatever crop lined both sides of the road and danced in the cool evening breeze.

Phil had looked at her strangely in the foyer of his parents' home and just now in the car, as if they'd been talking about something more than just the sleeping arrangements. Even though she stood in the center of the country, she felt as if she were trying to balance on a raft in the ocean, trying to anticipate the next wave that could take her under for good. Phil reached for her hand and led her toward the admittance gate. When she tried to pull her hand free, he held on tight. She thought she saw a hint of hurt in the frustrated look he spared her. How could that be? She was the one about to capsize and drown.

He pulled her to the side of the walkway to let the group behind them pass. "Look," he said in a whisper that had his breath tickling the side of her face. "I know you don't want to hold hands, but I guess we should have talked about this. If we're going to act like we're in love, you're going to have to be okay with me touching you."

I'm more than okay with you touching me, she wanted to say. It's when you stop that I'll have a problem. It's when the weekend is over and I can't stop thinking about you touching me is the problem. "I'm fine with it, Phil. I'm just…your parents are really nice. I guess I feel a little weird deceiving them like this."

"That's on me. I don't want you feeling guilty for doing me a favor."

Right. A favor. Holding hands and smoldering looks were just a side benefit, but nothing more. She needed to remember the purpose of the weekend and step up to the plate.

Maybe if she initiated the touching, if she played up the physical side of their pretend relationship, she wouldn't feel so adrift and needy. She desperately wanted to feel in control.

She held out her hand, sent him a flirtatious grin when he linked their fingers, turned, and made her way to the gate.

"Two, please," he said to the older woman manning the table.

"Phillip Williams," she cooed. "Didn't expect to see you here tonight."

"Hi, Betsy." He handed over a ten-dollar bill from his money clip. "I'm in town for my father's retirement party tomorrow night."

"Of course," she said. Margot scooted behind Phil as kids pushed forward with money in hand. "Looking forward to the big shin-dig." She cocked her head to the side and winked at Margot. "How is South Carolina?"

"Great," he said, ignoring a perfect opportunity to introduce Margot as his girlfriend. "How's Jimmy?"

"Go on in and see for yourself. He's starting tight end."

"I'll do that, Betsy. Good to see you."

He reached behind and grabbed Margot's hand, pulling her along until the base of the stairs where the path opened up to the concession stand. She figured if he wanted people to think he wasn't gay, the crowded line for concessions was just about the best spot.

"Do you want a drink?" he asked.

His eyes widened as she stepped slowly into him so their chests brushed. She let her fingers dance up his shirt and into his hair, pulling his head down. She wondered if he could feel her heart galloping in her chest and the roaring in her ears as his hands came around and grabbed her waist. She nipped at his bottom lip only once before his eyes darkened and sharpened on her face. She'd intended to tease him, to flirt and play the part of the moony-eyed girlfriend, until he lowered his head to kiss her softly over and over again as if he were drinking from a spring and he were parched.

A cluster of teens walked by. "Get a room," one of them said and giggled along the path.

She sagged bonelessly against him before remembering where she was and why she was there. She straightened her back and stared into his eyes. "Mission accomplished," she said after clearing her throat. "And we're not even in the stadium yet."

He jerked his head back as if she'd slapped him. "What? Oh." He swiped a hand over his face. "Sorry about that. My brain kind of clicked off for a minute."

"I thought that's what you wanted?"

He rubbed the back of his neck and settled his hands on his hips. "I'm not sure what I want anymore."

She could only stare up at him, the man she'd lusted after for three years, who seemed like he was seeing at her for the first time.

"Margot—"

"Phil?"

His head lurched sideways and his hands slipped from his hips to dangle at his side. A woman with dark, glossy hair, bright shining eyes, and two bags of popcorn in each hand stood staring at Phil as if he'd materialized in front of her. "Julianne."

"I...I assumed you'd be back for your dad's party. I wasn't expecting to see you tonight."

"Just got in this afternoon." He shook his head at her and kept shaking it like his neck was on springs. "You look..." Margot followed his gaze from her tennis shoes and well-worn jeans to her royal blue sweatshirt. "You look good, Julianne."

"You, too, Phil." She glanced at Margot, obviously waiting for an introduction.

When it became clear he wasn't going to do anything but stare at the woman, Margot stuck out her hand. "I'm Margot Manning, Phil's girlfriend." She tucked her hand away quickly, nodding toward the popcorn. "You obviously can't shake. Sorry."

"It's nice to meet you, Margot."

"So how have you been?" Phil asked, oblivious to his social faux pas. Margot had never seen him behave so awkwardly.

"Good. Kids are keeping us busy."

"I've heard they can do that."

"You heard right."

Margot couldn't stand the sight of them locked in a flirtatious stare, two people with a history and who, at the moment, only had eyes for each other. She backed away slowly and, when neither of them noticed, made a beeline for the bathroom.

Inside the stall, with the cheering crowd and flushing toilets singing in the background, she pondered the strange turn her life had taken. She'd never left the state of South Carolina, and here she sat in Cash, Illinois at a high school football game, trying to hold back tears of frustration. She looked at her watch. Had it really only been six hours since she'd stood in her house anticipating the weekend to come with excitement? She swallowed her emotions, washed and dried her hands, and walked out into the night, not sure where to find Phil or if he would have even noticed that she'd gone.

"There you are," he said from behind her. "I've been looking all over for you."

"Sorry." Her tone came out sharper than she'd intended, but she couldn't stand the way he was looking at her, as if she'd intentionally ditched him. "I had to use the bathroom."

"Why didn't you tell me where you were going?"

"I didn't think you'd even notice," she mumbled as she moved toward the field. The sooner they took their seats, the sooner their charade would be over and she could go to bed. The image of the pretty queen bed flashed through her mind and she realized her troubles were only beginning.

He grabbed her hand and led the way. "I don't know why you say that," he said over his shoulder. They inched up the teeming bleachers while Phil called greetings to practically everyone around them. Margot felt her cheeks heating under the curious stares of the crowd. He led her to the top corner of the stands where his mom and dad were already seated.

"We thought maybe you got lost." Judy leaned over Bo to give Margot a smile.

"The game's packed," Phil said in answer. He obviously wasn't going to mention his run in with Julianne.

"We're 7 and 3," Bo explained. "We might actually make the playoffs this year. Soloman's our biggest rival."

"Soloman used to be terrible," Phil shouted across Margot to his dad. "We crushed them every year."

"They've got a big tire plant there now." Bo reached for Judy's popcorn and she shooed his hand away. "It's a bigger school than it used to be."

Phil scanned the crowd, his eyes landing on Julianne and her family. "Yeah," he said only loud enough for her to hear. "A lot has changed."

Julianne sat a few rows down with a stocky man with thinning hair and broad shoulders. Between them were two boys with inky black hair. She spared a glance at Phil. He watched the four of them so intently he had a furrow between his brows. He was probably wondering the same thing as Margot. How had that guy snagged a cute girl like Julianne? From the way Phil stared, Margot knew the guy had stolen Julianne right out from under Phil's nose.

Judy passed the popcorn to Margot, who passed it to Phil. He took a handful and popped it in his mouth. "Did you want something from the concession stand?" he asked. "I'm sorry," he said. "I didn't even offer before we came up here."

"I'm fine," Margot said. If only that were true.

*** 

Phil stared at Julianne and Stan Waterston and the two boys between them. Except for a few extra pounds around her midsection and some lines around her eyes, Julianne looked the same as she did in high school. He would have recognized her anywhere. Stan, on the other hand, hadn't aged well. His bald spot shone in the field lights and he'd gained more than a few pounds. As the school's best linebacker, he'd always been thick, but with the passing years, he'd edged a little closer to pudgy. Julianne must have inherited her mother's gift in the kitchen.

As the second quarter ticked away on the scoreboard, he pondered his feelings about seeing her again. He'd heard about her marriage and the birth of her boys, but he'd never actually been face to face with her since the night she'd broken his heart. He'd always imagined them meeting again and laughing about the good times they'd shared together, thankful they'd parted ways before he'd done something stupid and proposed. He never imagined she'd sigh with relief that the rumors of his homosexuality weren't true. As if she had reason to doubt.

Julianne had never wanted to leave Cash or her family behind. She'd gone to college in St. Louis and come home every weekend while Phil had mended his wounds at Ball State and only come home for holidays, careful to avoid her. She let him go, she'd said all those years ago, so he could spread his wings and fly without the burden of a hometown girlfriend with marriage and kids on her mind. Phil couldn't imagine living in Cash, growing old with the same guys he went to high school with, going to games on

Friday nights and church every Sunday. She'd done the right thing in letting him go, but he always thought of her as the one that got away. Sitting in the stands, watching her and her husband and their kids, made him feel lucky to have been given the gift of freedom.

He could feel someone staring at him and turned his head in time to catch Margot's annoyed glare. He hadn't meant to press his mouth to hers after the little nip she'd given him. Her minty breath had swept over his face like an invitation and, before he could stop himself, he'd planted a kiss on those very appealing lips.

He hadn't meant to feel the little hitch and hum of anticipation like he usually did when he'd finally gotten his hands on a woman he…appreciated. He hadn't meant to forget it was Margot who stood before him, her breasts brushing his chest while his fingers dug into the soft silk of her hair. He certainly hadn't meant to elicit a moan from his ex-receptionist and pretend girlfriend as he took her lips again and again and again, as her hands gripped his arms and tugged him closer so their bodies met dangerously close in all the right places.

Off limits, he told himself as she shivered beneath the jean jacket in the cool October evening. He reached his arm around her shoulders and scooted her closer.

"You're cold," he said to her answering scowl. He leaned closer as a flyaway curl teased the skin of his cheek. "And we're supposed to be happy together."

"How in the world could I forget?" she whispered.

When he pulled back, he caught his mother's lips twitching as she jabbed his dad in the ribs.

"What?" his father asked. "I wasn't even reaching for the popcorn."

"Phil?" Margot said, drawing his attention back to her face and the stubborn line between her brows. "I'm not sure what you want from me. Are you mad about earlier?"

"When you kissed me?" he asked.

"When you kissed me," she stated.

"How could I be mad?" He tucked the curl behind her ear and watched it pop back into place. She blew it out of her eyes with a sexy pout. "You did exactly what I asked." And more. As she turned her head and watched the game, he wondered if he would he be able to stop if she did it again.

# CHAPTER 12

Judy pursed her lips as she pretended to watch the game and snuck glances at her oldest son and his "girlfriend." She'd thought, before dinner, that they might be in a real relationship, but now she wasn't so sure.

"What's wrong with you?" Bo asked. "Cash just scored and you didn't even move."

"Nothing," she said. She waved her head toward Phil and Margot. "What do you think about them?"

"I like her."

"I know you like her. What's not to like about her? I mean them as a couple?"

He leaned forward and then back. Judy felt his shoulders rise and fall at her side. "They look cute together."

"Do you think they're playing us?"

Bo leaned over again and smiled when Phil caught him looking. "I don't know. They're all snuggled up."

"Phil didn't know about her father."

"Huh?" he asked after he'd slapped his knee in frustration as Soloman's punt returner was finally brought down on Cash's 45-yard line.

"Margot said she didn't know her father and Phil didn't know. If they were in a relationship, he would know that, don't you think?"

"Maybe she doesn't like to talk about it."

"She told us," Judy stewed before looking over again. Phil held Margot tight. She could see affection on her son's face, but she couldn't tell if there was more. Maybe this whole experiment wasn't such a good idea after all.

"Why don't you just ask him if they're really dating or if he brought her just to quell the rumors?" Bo suggested.

"I can't do that." Judy sat up straight and waved at friend.

"Why not?"

"I'm not sure I want to know the answer."

***

Margot felt Phil stiffen in his seat before he abruptly rose and stared down at a man who could only be his brother. This must be Devon, she thought as the broad-shouldered man made his way through the crowd like a king through his minions. Devon and Phil favored each other with their dark hair and brown eyes, but when he finally reached the aisle where Phil stood glaring, Devon had to look up to his older brother.

"Phil," Devon said with a wary smile.

"Dev." Phil stared at his brother with narrowed eyes before reaching back to pull Margot to her feet. "This is my girlfriend, Margot. Margot," he motioned with his hand and poked Devon in the chest. "This is my baby brother, Devon."

Devon pinned Margot with a charming smile and his wide-set dimples flashed to life. "Margot. You sure are a pretty little thing."

"Thank you," she said. She couldn't imagine Phil referring to anyone in such a condescending manner.

"Where's Sheryl?" Phil asked.

"She's helping one of the cheerleaders. Some sort of hair emergency."

"Good," Phil said and took Devon's arm. "Then you won't mind running to the concession stand with me. Margot's thirsty and I'll need some help."

"I just got here, Philly. I think you can handle it."

Phil stepped in his path and refused to let him pass. "I insist."

Margot watched Phil drag Devon down the stairs and looked back at Judy and Bo. They both watched the scene play out with matching worried expressions on their faces. What in the world was Phil up to?

\*\*\*

"Let go of my arm and quit dragging me around like I'm eight," Devon hissed when they reached the bottom step. "What in the hell's your problem?"

Phil poked Devon in the chest. "You're my problem," he said and turned to walk past the concession stand, past the restrooms, and into the shadow of the bleachers. Devon followed without another word.

"What's this all about?" Dev asked.

"Why the hell did you start a rumor I'm gay? Do you have any idea how that makes me feel? How it makes mom and dad feel? For God's sake, Mom's got us sleeping together in the guest room."

"I didn't start any rumor, Phil. You're barking up the wrong tree."

"Then who did?"

Devon had his mouth clamped so tight, Phil could see a vein throbbing in his temple. "How do I know? And why would you blame me?"

Phil paced away before turning back to stare down his brother. "Who else had reason, huh? Who else even gives a shit?"

"You think I want to be known as the guy with the gay brother? Please. This is a small town and I've got a reputation to uphold."

Phil stared at his brother and watched the vein in his head throb and throb. When Devon began the telltale guilty shuffling of his feet, Phil knew he'd caught him red handed. "You're lying."

"Phil…"

"Just admit it was you," Phil said. "I know it was. You never could tell a lie to save your life."

"Fine," Devon sputtered. "I'll tell you the truth, but only so you know it wasn't me." He wiped his hands on his jeans and looked Phil in the eye. "It was Mom."

Phil chortled. "What? Jesus, Dev. I can't believe you'd throw your own mother under the bus to save your ass. You really are a prick."

"I'm not lying, Phil. Mom started this whole thing."

"That's crazy. Why would she start a rumor I'm gay?"

"She didn't start a rumor you're gay. She told you I'd heard rumors you're gay."

"Did you?" Phil asked.

"No. Mom lied to you so you'd bring someone home, and then she sent Dad over to the shop to tell me what she'd done and that's when things got a little out of hand."

"What do you mean, out of hand?"

"Well, you know how loud Dad is when he talks? There were people in the store and they overheard and it just kind of snowballed from there."

Phil paced away, paced back, and stopped in front of Devon with his hands on his hips. "Are you telling me that Mom lied about the rumor, Dad tried to explain the lie to you, someone overheard, and now what Mom said is true? People really do think I'm gay?"

Dev squinted his eyes as if mentally playing catch-up with the scenario Phil outlined. "Yeah, that sounds about right."

Phil could feel the anger spread from his head to his heart to his gut. His own mother. How could she? Phil grabbed Devon's shirt in his fist and lifted him to his toes so they were eye to eye. "You'd better be telling me the truth."

Devon waved his hands in the air. "I am. I swear."

Phil dropped him like a doll. He shook his head back and forth. "Just so I'd bring a woman home? What was she thinking? Does she have any idea the kind of stress I've been under? How hard it was to talk Margot into coming with me?"

"Hell, I know it sounds bad, but that cute little blonde ought to bring a quick death to the rumors. Just put on a little PDA, and everything's back to normal."

Great. Public displays of affection with the one woman he recently deemed off limits. Could his life get any better?

"Where'd you meet her?" Dev asked.

"She used to work for me."

"Nice. I like the curls. And the tits. Bet it was hell keeping your hands to yourself when she was your employee."

If only Devon knew how hard it was for him to keep his hands off her now. "I can't believe my own mother would do this to me. I don't even know what to say."

"Well, I'd give her a taste of her own medicine if I was you."

"What do you mean?"

Dev gave Phil his most mischievous smile. "You're sleeping in the guest room, right? Both of you?"

"I told you we are."

Devon chuckled and leaned up to Phil. "That bed squeaks like the devil. If you and the blonde go at it later, Mom and Dad are sure to hear through the wall."

"Her name's Margot." Phil jerked back to see the laugh in his brother's eyes. "How do you know the bed squeaks?"

"Sheryl and I spent the weekend with Mom and Dad when we had our floors redone. Wish someone had warned me."

Great. Now he not only had to worry about making a move on her in his sleep, but of moving in general. It would serve his mother right if she thought he and Margot had sex right under her nose. But he didn't know if he could face his parents in the morning if they thought he'd had sex in the next room.

"Come on," Dev said. "Let's get out of here before someone thinks we're a couple."

\*\*\*

Judy's hackles went up the minute Phil returned. He dragged Margot to her feet and asked if she were ready to go without looking his mother in the eye. Since Margot had been dodging Judy's questions about how she and Phil had met and how long they'd been dating, she wasn't surprised when the girl took off like a shot.

"We're heading home," Phil announced as Margot came to his side. "We'll see you back at the house."

Judy stood up and tried to smile. "Okay, honey. See you later." When they were halfway down the bleachers, she pivoted toward Devon. "Spill it, Dev. Every word."

"Huh?" Dev said. Cash had made a first down and the volume from the crowd had increased tenfold.

"What did he say to you?"

"Who? Phil? He thought I was the one who started the gay rumor, thank you very much. As if he didn't hate me enough already."

"Your brother doesn't hate you," Judy insisted. "When it comes right down to it, the gay rumor is your fault."

"Excuse me?" he said after the Cash quarterback was sacked for a loss. "I'm not the one who started the rumor."

"It was never meant to be a rumor. Just a pretend rumor."

"It's not my fault the Reynolds' boy overheard dad telling me about your pretend rumor. I wasn't about to let anyone think it was me."

"So what did you tell him?" she asked.

"I told him I didn't know who started the rumor or why. Oh," his eyes twinkled with delight. "And I warned him about the squeaky guest room bed."

Judy flinched. She'd never forget the night Devon and Sheryl stayed in the guest room and she and Bo had to listen to their son and his wife having sex through the wall. How much worse would it be to hear her unmarried son and his maybe girlfriend having sex?

# CHAPTER 13

They had pie at home with a fire crackling in the parlor. Phil had called it the parlor, as if he lived in a Greek mansion she'd only read about in books. He carried their plates in along with a glass of wine.

"Wine and pie," she said when he handed her the plate. "And ice cream. Thank you."

"It's an odd combination, but one that appeals to all my tastes."

"Mmmm," she said after taking a nibble. "All of mine, as well."

His fork stopped half way to his mouth and he stared at her from across the small space between their chairs. She couldn't read his expression in the dim light, but she knew he looked incredibly handsome in his socks, jeans, and flannel shirt. Somehow the outfit that had looked so silly on him that morning seemed to fit him like a glove by nightfall.

"What's wrong?" she asked.

"Hummm? Oh, nothing." He shoveled a bite into his mouth and looked away.

She could read him better, had read his moods for years from the safe distance of obscurity. But now, seated intimately in the cozy setting with his eyes on her and their legs dangerously close, she couldn't have said what had caused him to go silent. "I like Cash," she said to break the suddenly uncomfortable silence. "Downtown is picturesque, even when everyone was at the game."

"There's something to be said for small towns." He sipped from the wine he'd bought at the liquor store on their ride home. "Not too much different from Echo."

"I don't know," Margot said. "Echo's a beach town. There's a whole different feel. It's…laid back and go with the flow. Andover is upscale elegance disguised as small town. Cash is just good old fashioned Americans trying to make a living."

"You don't think people in Echo or Andover are trying to make a living?"

"Of course they are, but some of the people—most of the people—are outsiders. They're drifters who've come to the coast to find a better life or one that's not so rushed. This feels more rooted, I guess."

"That's because the earth is harder here. It's hard to make roots in sand."

"Is that why you came to Echo?" she asked. "So your roots wouldn't stick?"

He settled his plate on the side table and cupped his glass between both hands. When he stretched his legs out, his feet brushed hers. "That's an interesting question. I couldn't wait to get out of here and not because this is a bad place. What you said about roots is exactly right. People who stay here too long never leave."

"And you wanted to leave?"

"I had to leave. There was a whole world out there to explore and I didn't want to get tied up in the town I'd grown up in, doing the same thing with the same people for the rest of my life."

"They seem like good people to me."

"Oh, they are. I forget sometimes just how good when I'm gone for too long. They're some of the best."

"Why Echo?" she asked. This was a part of him she didn't know, couldn't know because of their surface relationship. She could feel Cash taking root in her heart, and yet she wanted to know more, needed to know more about the man who stirred feelings inside of her.

"I met Danny the summer before I graduated. I came down with a friend who had a house on Sullivan's Island. It was so different from Cash. I remember the first time I got out of the car and smelled the salt in the air." He took a sip and stared at the fire. "Danny and I just clicked, ya know. I knew in one afternoon that I'd be back, that we'd end up working together."

"Whose idea was the business?"

"Both of ours. I made the business plan, got the loan, set our short term and long term goals, did all the marketing." He set his glass down and pulled his feet back under the chair.

"I've never heard anyone speak of you two, professionally, as anything other than the best."

He turned his head and stared at her. "Really?"

"Yeah. I'd say your business planning paid off. Most folks didn't take Danny seriously until you came along."

"And I couldn't have gotten anywhere around Echo or Andover without his local connections. We're a good team." His expression turned serious. "We're going to miss you at the office. I'm going to miss you."

Margot's heart skipped a beat. Did he really mean it? No, of course not. She had to stop thinking his looks and his words meant anything more than gratitude. "Change is hard. Rebecca is—"

"Not you, but we'll muddle through. I can't exactly ask you to give up your nursing career to be our receptionist."

"Speaking of nursing." Margot stood up and gathered her plate and wine glass in her hands. "I'd better look over some notes before I go to bed."

"Margot?" Phil followed her into the kitchen with his plate and glass. He took her plate from her hand and placed them in the sink. Normally he would have put the dishes in the dishwasher, but not now. He was still mad at his mother. "I need to tell you something."

"Okay..."

"Devon told me my mom made up the rumor about me being gay just so I'd bring someone home."

"Your mom? Are you sure you believe him?"

"Yes. I do."

She couldn't imagine Judy lying to Phil about anything. "Well. I guess the jig is up." She knew she was in too deep when knowing the charade was over made her feel disappointed instead of glad. No more holding hands, smoldering looks, and scorching kisses. "Are you going to tell her you know? Confess the truth?"

"I don't know what I'm going to do."

She noted the gleam in his eye and the way his hands fisted at his sides. "You look ready to enact revenge."

"Dev suggested we 'go at it' in the squeaky guest room bed."

She felt the blood drain from her face and pool between her legs. "What?"

"Nevermind." He ran his hand down his face and shook his head. "It's been a long day."

Margot needed to get out of Cash. She needed a little breathing room and a clean break from Phil before she did or said something stupid. "Why don't I see if I can catch a flight out in the morning? It sounds like you and your parents have some things to discuss."

"Leave?" he asked. "Why would you leave?"

"Phil, the rumors aren't real. You know it was your mom, and she can probably tell we're not dating. Why would I stay?"

"I just assumed you'd stay through the weekend." He stepped toward her and shoved his hands into the front pockets of his jeans. "I actually need you to stay."

She couldn't help it. Her breath caught in her throat and her pulse quickened as he stared down at her. Did he want her to stay because he felt a connection with her? Was the memory of their kiss branded on his heart the way his was branded on hers? "You do?"

"There's a bit more to tell. When my dad told Dev about the rumor, a customer at Dev's shop overheard and now the rumors are real. People do think I'm gay."

Stupid, stupid, stupid. How could she think their kiss and the cozy conversation by the fire had meant anything more to him than playing a role? "Oh, well, I guess I can stay. If people think you're gay."

"I'm sorry, Margot."

"Why are you sorry?" She looked down and began pulling at the ends of her scarf. She felt so transparent, she couldn't look him in the eye. "Nothing's changed. We'll pretend to be dating this weekend like we planned."

"Everything's changed. My mom...what she did. It's so deceitful. I can't believe she had it in her to lie to me like that."

"She wants to know about your life, Phil. You obviously haven't told her much about South Carolina. She practically grilled me at the game."

"She did?"

"While you and Dev were gone."

"Okay, maybe I haven't been very open about my life there, but there hasn't been much to tell. Like you pointed out, I've dated a lot of women. No one I'd bring home or even mention on the phone." He leaned back against the counter. "God, that doesn't speak well of me, does it?"

She shouldn't feel pity for him in a time of crisis, not when he'd pounded a stake through her heart. But damn it, she did. "You're a young, attractive, successful architect. You have every right to date whomever you want, whenever you want."

"I haven't been in a relationship—a real one—since high school."

"Julianne?"

"Yeah." He sighed.

Damn him, she felt tempted to move closer, rub his arm, try to wipe away the puppy dog look from his face. She stayed put.

"Do you think I'm emotionally immature?" he asked.

"Ahh, well..."

"Nevermind. Don't answer that." He pushed away from the counter and stood up straight. "I'm just confused. And pissed off. My mother put me in a bad position, and now I've put you in a bad position. I feel terrible that I dragged you half way across the country over some stupid farce."

"Phil." She did move toward him when she saw him working up a head of steam. She knew he'd reach full boil soon, and she suspected his parents would be back any minute. "I'm fine with this. What's done is done. I don't think your mom meant to ruin your reputation. It sounds like things just snowballed out of control." Which would explain the worried look on his parents faces when Phil dragged Devon away at the game. "I'm here, and tomorrow at the party, we'll put an end to the gay rumors once and for all."

They both turned toward the front of the house at the sound of tires on the drive. "They're home," he said with a grimace.

She grabbed his arm as he strode into the foyer. "Phil, wait. I think you need to calm down before you face her. Trust me, you can't take back the words you say when you're upset and those tend to be the ones that hit the hardest."

"She deserves to hear what her prank has done."

"She won't hear anything if you're upset." She dragged him to the stairs. "Please, come up to bed, sleep on this, and talk to her in the morning."

"Margot..."

"You're too upset to be rational, Phil. Trust me."

He sighed and followed her up the stairs and into the small bedroom. She closed the door just as the front door opened. "See," he whispered, pointing to the bed. "This pisses me off, too. One bed for the two of us when I promised you'd have your own room."

"It's okay, Phil."

"It's not okay." He pivoted and waved his arms in the air. "I'm going to go talk to her now, clear this whole thing up, and sleep on the couch."

Margot moved as quickly as she could, throwing her body against the door. "I won't let you do it."

"Margot, I'm fine. I'm calm. But I won't be able to sleep with all this hanging between us. I'm going to go talk to her."

"No, you're not. You're upset and you're ready to blow. Remember when you lost it with the Fire Marshall over the permit for the ed center?"

91

"That was a pissing match because Danny used to date his wife. I abhor that kind of professional misconduct and I let him have it."

"Exactly, and in letting him have it, you almost ended up in jail."

"I got the permit, didn't I?"

It was time to shut him down before he stormed out of the room and changed his relationship with his mom forever. "Two weeks before my mom died, I yelled at her for keeping something from me. I was so mad at her, and I said terrible, hurtful things that I never would have said if I hadn't been so upset. I'll never forget the way she looked at me. I would give anything to be able to go back and change what I did, what I said."

She tucked the painful memory away as she watched the anger leak out of him the way air escapes from an untied balloon. She'd hit the bull's-eye with her confession and felt the sting every bit as much as Phil.

"I'm sorry, Margot."

She held up her hands. If he touched her now, she might lose it. "Just promise me you won't do anything tonight. I'm not saying what she did was right, but I'm sure she had her reasons. Remorse is a very heavy burden, Phil. Trust me, save yourself and your mom the trouble and wait until you can talk about this rationally."

\*\*\*

Phil stuck his head under the spray of hot water, his mind full of Margot. With one painful admission, she'd taken all his anger toward his mother and brushed it aside. Now his heart ached for her and the burden she carried. What had her mother kept from her? What had she said to her mother, and how did she live with the guilt when it was written so painfully on her face? She'd looked as fragile as glass when she stopped him from confronting his mother in a fit of rage.

He turned off the faucet and reached for a towel. Damn it, the woman was getting to him and he didn't like it one bit. He should have taken a cold shower to ease the anticipation building as he brushed his teeth and pictured her waiting for him in bed wearing the silky lingerie he spied in her suitcase earlier. Stop, he ordered himself. She was his friend. She was dating one of his friends and a client. He couldn't do anything to jeopardize their relationship no matter how much he wanted to.

His parents' door was closed and a dim light shone through the crack. It would serve them right if he did throw caution and good sense out the window and marched into the guest room and seduced Margot. But no matter how much he wanted to get even, no matter how much he wanted to unleash this newfound desire, he knew he couldn't face himself in the morning if he took advantage of Margot.

With a sigh, he eased the door to the guest room open. She'd gotten into bed and stacked some pillows behind her head. She pulled the covers up and tucked them tightly under her arms so all he could see were the short sleeves of a green shirt. He should have felt relieved instead of disappointed. With a mental head slap, he entered the room wearing an undershirt and worn, flannel sleeping pants. Her head jerked up from the notes on her lap.

"Feel better?" she asked.

The sleepy slowness of her voice had the hair on the back of his neck prickling. He averted his eyes from the bed and looked at the stack of books piled on the bedside. "Yeah, thanks."

He picked a book from the nightstand and pulled back the comforter and sheet, careful not to look under the covers at what Margot may or may not have on. He slid between the chilled sheets and groaned when his feet bumped the footboard from a semi-reclined position. "Great," he mumbled.

"I don't take up much room," she said. "Stretch out as much as you need."

If he stretched out, he'd be all over her. If he were all over her, he'd want to be inside her. He shifted and lifted his knees to hide what the thought of that did to his body. "I'm fine," he lied.

She piled her notes on the nightstand and turned off her light. "Read as long as you want." She scooted beneath the covers so that all he could see was her head. The bed squeaked loudly when she turned away from him and snuggled against her pillow. He tortured himself by following the outline of her body, the swell of her backside, her hair rioting across the pillow. Every part of him ached to touch her, so he turned back to the book and tried to concentrate on the words.

After rereading the same paragraph three times, he set the book aside, turned off the light, and tried to lay flat. His knees buckled. He turned onto his side, away from temptation, and his feet slid out from under the covers and dangled over the edge of the bed. Within minutes, his feet were freezing and he was forced to roll over. He'd just stretched out his legs in Margot's direction when he felt the bed shake. From the sounds she made, Phil thought Margot was crying.

"Margot?" he asked, gently touching her shoulder.

She rolled over and let out a snorting laugh. In the light coming in from under the blinds, he could see her propped up on her elbows and the outline of her breasts when the blankets slipped to her waist. "I'm sorry," she said through strangled breaths. "But this bed is just awful. We don't have to do anything more than breathe in here for your mom and dad to think we're having sex."

"It is awful, isn't it? I'm tempted to keep moving so my parents don't think I'm a one-pump chump."

In the silence that followed, he thought better of what he'd said until she snorted again and gave a full out belly laugh. How had he ever thought her laugh was anything but music? "It would serve them right to think we were...having fun in here."

He sat up and gave a couple of quick bounces on the bed. The rhythmic squeaking started Margot giggling again. She sat up. "Do you want me to throw in a few 'oh baby's'?"

He was rock hard in two seconds flat. He stopped bouncing. "Uh..."

She swatted his arm. "If you stop now, they are going to think you're a one-pump chump." She motioned with her hand for him to keep going as she began bouncing on the bed. "Oh, Phil," she moaned. "Yes, baby, yes, just like that."

He could do nothing more than watch her, the way her breasts jiggled under her shirt, the curve of her back, the pivoting of her hips as she pounded again and again against the mattress. Her throaty whispers floated over him like a fog, pulling him deeper and deeper under her spell. He'd never been more aroused than watching Margot flop fully clothed on the bed like a porn star in the making.

When she realized he wasn't helping, she abruptly stopped. "Sorry," she whispered. "I got a little carried away."

"No, no, you were perfect," he said. Every muscle in his body was as tight as a drum. "That'll show them."

She fell against the pillow and threw her hands on her face. "I'm such an idiot. I'm sorry."

"For what?" he asked. He reached over and peeled her hand away. "I'm the one who started it."

"And I'm the one who took it too far." She groaned and the sound only made his pulse beat louder in his groin. "Now your parents really do think we had sex. How am I going to face them in the morning?"

"Margot. They're the ones who insisted we sleep in the same room, in the same bed. There isn't a man alive who could keep his hands off you in this bed."

She turned her head so they were face to face. He felt every breath she took sweep over his face. "You haven't touched me, Phil. We just pretended."

"I'm having a hell of a time pretending I don't want to."

She leaned up on her elbow and lifted her hand to her mouth, right where he wanted his lips to be. "You..."

"Go to sleep, Margot, before I do something we'll both regret."

She eased back into the pillow and stared straight up at the ceiling. He hoped the sheen from her eyes was just the reflection from the moon's glare and not tears. "Okay. Good night, Phil."

He slipped down, stretching his feet toward her, careful not to make contact even as the heat from her body called to him like a beacon in the night. "Good night, Margot. Sweet dreams."

# CHAPTER 14

Phil was gone when Margot woke up with the sun on her face. She smoothed her hand over the imprint his body had left on the bed and felt the chill all the way to her heart. *Go to sleep, Margot, before I do something we'll both regret.* His words, the hungry longing she'd heard in every syllable, zipped like lightning through her already throbbing body. He'd wanted her. If he'd had her, if he'd given in to the desire that had thrummed between them the night before, he'd have regretted it. Not because his parents were in the next room, not because he'd taken advantage of a situation, but because it was her. His receptionist. His friend. The girl who'd done him a favor. And now, because she knew him so well, she knew he already had regrets for what almost happened between them.

She threw back the covers and let her legs dangle from the side of the bed. She didn't hear any noise from anywhere in the house. If only she could click her heels three times and be back home in her room in Echo with nothing more to face than hours of study time and a walk along the beach. Because she couldn't click her heels and go home, she got up and gathered her things from the suitcase and went to the bathroom for a shower.

The pipes groaned when she started the water and reminded her of the night before. Not only did she have to face Phil and his conscience, but his parents who thought they'd had sex in their guest room. What had she been thinking, bouncing on the bed like some adolescent schoolgirl playing tricks on adults? No wonder Phil thought of her as a child. It had started out so innocently, bouncing on the bed with the sound of his laughter in her ears. Until she'd gotten carried away and maybe, just maybe, she'd kept going just to show him she wasn't a kid. To show him what he was missing, to show him she was a woman with desires and needs and that, yes, she liked sex and that having it would be fun and real and exciting.

She let the water hit her face and thought of her mother. She would be ashamed of Margot, luring a man to her bed and acting on her desire without a second thought to the consequences. Only Margot's behavior was worse because she'd condemned her mother for doing the same and then turned around and did it herself. "Like mother, like daughter, mom," she mumbled to herself. "The apple doesn't fall far from the tree."

***

The air smelled so achingly familiar, a mix of grass and dirt and clean. Phil ran along the dirt road surrounded by corn and the sound of a tractor in the distance. He could see the plume of dust it created along the edge of the horizon. It felt good to stretch his legs and his lungs after a long and sleepless night. He knew he needed to turn around, but he couldn't bring himself to go back home and face...everything. His mother. Margot.

Margot.

He quickened his pace as his filthy mind recalled images of her silhouette bouncing on the bed, her throaty moans like tentacles trying to pull him under. Stop, he ordered himself. Stop thinking about Margot. Stop wanting her. Just stop. He reached the end of the Harper's fence line and knew he had to turn around or he wouldn't have the stamina to make it home. Not on an empty stomach and tired legs.

His mother was sure to be awake when he returned, making breakfast in the kitchen, acting as if she hadn't started a rumor that had led him to almost making love to Margot. Except his mom probably thought he had made love to Margot. Maybe he should've made love to Margot. At least the guilt he was sure to feel when he got home and faced his parents would be real. God knows he'd feel less tense.

If his mother gave him grief about last night, he'd happily point out that her lies that had put them together in the first place. He still couldn't believe she'd lied to get him to bring someone home. Okay, he didn't share much information with her about his love life. The truth was, he didn't have much of one. He dated. A lot.

But looking back on his years in South Carolina, he realized his dating felt kind of like the interviewing he'd done last week with the candidates who'd wanted Margot's job. He'd been interviewing women for the job of his girlfriend. And none of them, in eight years, had gotten more than four or five dates in before things fizzled. What did it say about him that he couldn't sustain a relationship? That he didn't find anything in all the women he'd dated appealing enough to have a long-term relationship?

He felt sick with doubt and confusion as he rounded the drive to his house. Phil heaved a sigh of relief that his dad's truck was gone. Good. At least he didn't have to face more than one set of condemning eyes when he stopped stretching and worked up the courage to go inside. The sweat on his skin began to cool and he knew he couldn't stall any longer. From the foyer, he heard his mother in the kitchen, humming along to the radio while she prepared what smelled like either pancakes or waffles. He hoped it was waffles.

He heard the shower running above and knew Margot was using the bathroom. He may as well face his mother without an audience.

"Hey," he said from the threshold of the kitchen. His mother jumped in surprise.

"Oh, Phil," she clutched her hand to her chest. "You scared me."

"Sorry." He opened the refrigerator, pulled out the orange juice, and poured himself a tall glass.

"You're up early," she said.

Was it him, or was there a hint of an accusation in her tone? "I like to run before it gets too hot."

She chuckled. "You've been in the South too long if you think it's going to get hot in Cash in October."

He shrugged. "Guess you're right."

"You sleep okay?"

Here we go, he thought. "Like a baby," he lied and stared at her back, willing her to turn around and challenge him on the morals of banging his girlfriend under her roof. But she stayed facing the wall and filled up the waffle iron with a ladle. She wasn't going to make this easy.

"How about you, Mom? How did you and Dad sleep?"

"With those pills Doc Martin gave me for my back, I sleep like the dead. Your dad must not have slept well because he sure was in a grumpy mood this morning."

"Where'd he go so early on a Saturday?"

"He's helping Shane with the combine. His sweet corn has to be harvested early in the morning."

He leaned against the counter and heard the pipes shut off upstairs. The thought of a wet Margot in the bathroom didn't help. "That's something you don't hear much in South Carolina."

"What are the crops down there?" she asked.

"Hummm," he said. "Tobacco, of course. And maybe cotton? I'm not sure. Margot would know. She's lived there all her life."

His mother closed the lid on the waffle iron and turned to face him. "I like her, Philly. She's pretty, and sweet, and you should see the way she looks at you."

He choked on his orange juice. "What do you mean, the way she looks at me?"

"The way a woman looks at the man she loves."

"Mom," he cleared his throat. "I...Margot and I...we're not, I mean, we are, but..."

She swatted him with the dishtowel she'd pulled from her shoulder. "Oh, Phil. Just that right there says it all."

"Says what?"

"That you're in love, silly. I'm glad you brought her home so your dad and I could meet her."

He felt the blood rise from his chest to his neck to his face. "So I guess it was worth it? Lying to me so that I'd bring Margot home?"

Her face went slack and then filled with bright pink patches on her cheeks. She wouldn't look him in the eye. "What are you talking about?"

"I know what you did. I know you lied about the gay rumors and I also know that now everyone in Cash thinks I'm gay because Dad and Devon couldn't keep their mouths closed."

"Wha...who told you?"

"Why does it matter? Is it true?"

"Oh, honey, I didn't want to lie to you."

"But you did, and now everyone thinks I'm gay! Do you know how that makes me feel?"

"Not too great, I'd imagine."

"Not half as bad as knowing my own mother started the rumor." He slammed the glass on the counter and she jumped.

"I never meant for it to leave the family, I swear. Phil, you're just so closed mouthed about your life down there. You never tell me anything about how you spend your time and who with. I wanted to know that you weren't cutting yourself off from women the way you did when Julianne dumped you."

"I never cut myself off from women. What gave you that idea?"

"You went through all four years of college and through grad school without ever dating anyone more than a week or two. I'm your mother and it broke my heart thinking of you all alone."

"I haven't been all alone, in college or down South. God, do you want a list of the women I've been involved with? Would that make you happy?"

"No, I don't want a list, but maybe just a name every now and again. I worry about you."

"I'm fine, Mom. I'm dating. I see women."

"Well, obviously. Your dad and I really like Margot."

The mention of her name, the pretense of what brought them to Cash, slapped him in the face. He wasn't any better than his mother, lying to her about Margot and the nature of their relationship. But could he admit they weren't a couple when he had her over the ropes? They weren't a couple, of course, but they weren't exactly just friends, either. "I'll bring women home to meet you when and only when I'm ready. I don't appreciate being bullied into bringing someone home simply because you're too stubborn to ask who I'm dating."

"Would you have told me?"

Probably not, he admitted to himself. "Of course I would," he lied. "I'm not a social hermit. And despite what all of Cash thinks, I'm not gay."

"I'm sorry, Phil. It was wrong for me to lie to you and I feel terrible that it got out. But if it makes you feel any better, I think people don't believe it anymore after seeing you and Margot together. You really do make a lovely couple."

"Yeah, we're just lovely." He carried the glass to the sink. "I'm going to take a shower," he said. "And, Mom?"

She looked at him with pleading eyes.

"Your waffles are burning."

***

Margot reluctantly turned off the water. She couldn't hide out in the shower all day long. She dried off, applied her scented moisturizer, and reached for her clothes, only to realize she'd left her bra and underwear in the room. "Great," she murmured and wrapped the plush cotton towel around her body while her hair dripped in her eyes. She scooped her clothes from the counter and tip toed across the hall to the guest room.

She sucked in her breath when she entered the room and Phil stood by the bed in running shorts, sopping his brow with the shirt he'd just whipped off. His chiseled chest gleamed in the bright morning sun.

"Hey," he said when he saw her. He eyed the towel she held against her body and then quickly looked away. "Any hot water left?"

"Plenty." She eased past him to where her suitcase sat atop the luggage rack. Her bra and panties were on top of the bed right where she'd left them, right next to where Phil stood. "How was it?"

"What?" he asked without looking up.

"The run. How was your run?"

"Good." He gathered a pair of jeans and a long-sleeved golf shirt from his bag and walked to the door. "You can go ahead and get dressed. I'm going to catch a shower."

"Okay," she said to his retreating back. Thankfully he closed the door behind him. She slumped against the wall and let out the breath she'd been holding. "Wow." She'd almost dropped the towel at the sight of him standing bare-chested by the bed where they'd almost made love. Just when she thought she couldn't get any more attracted to him, she had to walk in and see his goods. "One more night," she told herself. "Only one more night."

# CHAPTER 15

"What's wrong with you?" Dev asked Phil after Sheryl and his mom had left to decorate the Legion for the night's party. Phil rubbed his stuffed belly and eyed the mountain of dishes Margot was washing across the kitchen.

"Nothing."

"I knew it," Dev said. "I knew you wouldn't have the guts to nail your girlfriend with mom and dad in the next room."

"Shut up, Dev."

Devon looked over his shoulder at Margot. "I don't know how you managed to keep your hands off that sweet little thing. I'd have made a dent in the wall."

Phil punched Dev in the shoulder. Hard. "Eyes forward, Fuckwad."

Dev rubbed his shoulder. "That hurt."

"Good." Did Margot's hips have to sway back and forth in her not-too-tight, not-too-loose jeans as she scrubbed bacon grease from the griddle? He'd been at half-mast since she'd walked into the bedroom wearing only a towel and smelling like almonds. He loved the smell of almonds. "Quit looking at her ass."

"Make me," Dev said and shoved back from the table just in time to miss Phil's fist. "I know how to rectify the situation. You can thank me later."

Phil watched as Devon walked over to lean against the counter where Margot had begun loading the dishwasher. "Margot, have you ever seen horses breed?"

Oh no. He wouldn't.

103

"Um, no," Margot said. She shoved her hair out of her eyes with her wrist and only managed to get soap bubbles in her hair.

"You're in luck, little lady." He looked at his watch. "You and Philly come on over to my place at three this afternoon. I'm breeding my prize stud. It's a sight you'll never forget."

Margot looked back at Phil with a question in her eyes. "I've really got to study this afternoon, Devon, but thanks for the offer."

"Now, listen," Dev continued as if Margot hadn't already turned him down. "When will you ever get the chance to experience this again? I'm going to have to insist. In fact, I'll be personally insulted if you and Phil don't come over." He pushed away from the counter and scooped his keys off the table. "Three o'clock, sharp. Don't be late."

\*\*\*

Margot slid into the rental car at ten 'til three with a nervous flutter in her belly. Phil had avoided her all day, which was good because she'd gotten a lot of studying done when she hadn't been obsessing about where he was and what he was doing. At a quarter to three, she'd found him in the parlor, pacing back and forth in front of the fireplace.

"Are we going to Dev's?" she asked.

He glanced up at the clock on the mantle. "Uh, I don't think it's a very good idea."

"He seemed really adamant about us going, and to be honest, I could use a break." She stretched her aching back. "There're only so many arterial gas and blood loss calculations I can handle in one afternoon."

He eyed her warily. "Are you sure you want to go? We could get some ice cream or take a walk or something."

She shrugged. Ice cream and walks sounded a little too intimate to her. The less time they spent alone, the better. "I'd kinda like to see the horses."

"Margot," Phil said, drawing her attention back to the present. They drove through town and out past the high school to where buildings gave way to acres of crops. "Horse breeding is kind of physical."

"Well, yeah. I'm almost a nurse, Phil. I know the technicalities of breeding."

"What I mean is," he continued after clearing his throat. Margot noticed his hands fisting the wheel as if he were driving a stock car race. "Sometimes the horses get a little wild. If you're not used to it, the sight can be a little intimidating."

"What am I, a wimp? You're only making me want to see it more. Besides, Dev would be personally insulted if we didn't show up." She looked out the window as they passed a large piece of farm equipment along the road. "Is your brother always so dramatic?"

"Unfortunately, yes."

He turned into a drive marked by a sign that said, "Williams Breeding" with a picture of a large stallion. "What kind of horses does he breed?"

"Mostly Morabs. There's a therapy facility in the area that prefers that breed."

"I don't know much about horses, but I've never heard of Morabs."

"It's a mix between an Arabian and a Morgan. They're good horses."

They found Dev in a corral next to a large barn behind his modest home. He held the lead on a large brown horse that danced excitedly around the pen.

"There you are," Dev shouted as they approached. "I started to think you weren't coming."

"Where's the mare?" Phil asked.

"In the barn. We've had her under lights since the days have gotten shorter."

"What does that mean?" Margot asked.

"Horses usual breeding season is spring or summer when the days are longer," Phil answered.

"When we want to breed off-season, we keep the mares inside with the lights on to stimulate the season and get them to ovulate," Dev explained as he brought the fidgeting stallion to the gate. "You ready for the show?"

Margot glanced at Phil. He looked like he was heading into a funeral. "Yep," she said when he didn't answer.

"You two go on ahead into the barn, but stay back near the corner out of the way. This guy's gonna get real excited when he gets inside and knows what's coming."

Phil led Margot into the well-lit barn. A man in jeans, a t-shirt, and ball cap held a beautiful gray horse in the corner. Her tail had been braided and her mane appeared neatly groomed. The cement floor looked neat and sterile. The scene reminded Margot of an operating room with the smell of chemicals in the air.

"Why does it smell like cleaner in here?" she asked.

"Dev's hand has already cleaned the mare." He pointed to the drain in the corner where the floor looked freshly wet. "It cuts down on infection during conception."

The sound of hoofs on the floor drew Margot's attention as the stallion pranced into the barn, his head high, and went straight to the gray horse. Margot watched as the brown horse sniffed the gray horse in the face and then began nipping along her mane. When the stallion swung around, Margot caught her first glimpse of his organ. "Oh, my," she said. "He's rather well endowed."

Phil chuckled beside her. "Yes, they do tend to put us humans to shame."

The stallion went behind the gray, who seemed to bristle at the poking and nipping. Dev's helper held tight to the lead, keeping her in place. The gray lifted her tail and the stallion poked her privates with his nose, drinking in her scent.

"He's checking to make sure she's ready," Phil explained.

"Always a good idea." Margot couldn't take her eyes off the stallion. Her heart beat in her chest and her muscles went lax. The smell of sex was overwhelming. She took a step back when the stallion reared up to mount the gray. The feel of Phil's hand on her back was like setting a match to kindling. "Oh…"

The stallion entered the gray. After a handful of valiant thrusts, he rested his head against her mid-section as if reveling in the afterglow. He pulled out and Margot gasped. The end of his member was hugely engorged. Dev led the horse to the cleaning area and tossed some water from a cleaning bucket onto the stallion's shrinking organ and then back toward the entrance where Phil and Margot stood.

"What'd ya think?"

Margot could barely think through the sexual haze. Was it wrong to be turned on by watching horses mate? When she turned to look at Phil, he gave her one long stare. His pupils were huge. Good Lord, he was as turned on as she was. "Um, it was quicker than I thought it would be."

Dev laughed. "No fuss, no muss with these guys." He slapped Phil on the shoulder. "I've got to see to the big stud here. I'll see you guys tonight at the party."

Phil waved to Dev's helper and led Margot out to the rental. She felt loose and tingly and if he touched her in the small confines of the car, she was liable to go off like a firecracker. Now she understood Phil's reluctance. He opened her door and she slid inside, hoping the smell of sex hadn't followed along with them. He walked around the back of the car and got in beside her.

"You up for some ice cream now?" he asked.

There hadn't been anyone at home when they'd left and she felt sure he was reluctant to go home to an empty house. "Ice cream sounds good."

*** 

Phil kept his eyes on the road and tried to calculate the miles from Cash to Echo if they had driven, the miles from Cash to Los Angeles, the miles from Cash to Chicago, anything to get his mind off of Margot and the way she'd looked at him after watching the horses mate. He shouldn't have brought her, he should have insisted they go for a walk or go into town or do anything other than go to Dev's. Hell, he may as well have suggested they watch a little porn together. Cash to Indianapolis, he ordered himself to calculate.

"Where are we going?" Margot asked. Was it his imagination or did her voice sound different? Throaty and sexy as hell. He kept his eyes on the road.

"The Dairy Barn."

"We just passed it, Phil, unless there's another one closer to home."

"Shit," he mumbled and put on his signal to turn around at the grocery store.

There were only a few cars in the parking lot and a smattering of people in the restaurant. Phil ordered two soft serve cones and led Margot to a booth along the window. After watching her take the first lick, he realized he should have gotten them both a sundae. He forced his eyes away from her tongue and looked around the Dairy Barn.

"Did you hang out here as a kid?" Margot asked.

"Oh, yeah. This place was a staple of my diet for eighteen years."

"It's good," she said. He tortured himself and watched her lick the cone into a phallic shape. She hadn't put on lots of makeup today and her corkscrew hair rained across her shoulders. She looked like Margot, the real Margot. He liked the way her freckles dotted the bridge of her nose and the crazy mass of her hair. He couldn't remember what he'd ever found so unappealing about her looks. She stopped licking when she realized he was staring at her. "Your ice cream is melting."

"What?"

"Your ice cream." She pointed to his cone, dripping over his hands and onto the table.

"Oh."

She hopped up and brought a stack of napkins back to the table, taking a seat next to him on the small booth. "Give me your cone," she ordered.

He handed it to her and began wiping his hands. His cone continued to melt over Margot's hand. He reached for his cone at the same time she licked the ice cream from her fingers. When her tongue touched his thumb, he jolted in the seat. "I'll take it now," he said. "As a matter of fact, let's finish these in the car. We'd better get back so we can get ready for the party. Mom's probably going to need some help."

"Okay, sure." She scooted out of the booth and tossed the napkins in the trash receptacle next to their table. He was eye-level with her bottom and nearly groaned. How in the hell was he going to keep his hands off her tonight?

The only thing he knew for sure was that Devon was going to pay for this later.

# CHAPTER 16

Judy watched Phil and Margot enter the Legion Hall together and felt the corners of her lips twitch into a smile. What a stunning couple they made, him in his dark gray suit and her in a ruby-red, belted strapless chiffon dress. She'd pulled her hair up in a twist. Phil looked uncomfortable as he searched the room she and Sheryl had spent all day decorating with streamers, balloons, and a huge banner that said, "Congratulations, Bo." She walked between the tables set around the dance floor to catch their attention.

"Phil," she called. "You two look wonderful. Margot, I just love your dress."

"Thank you, Judy. You look beautiful," the girl said, clutching her wrap and the small black purse she carried.

"I've got the family sitting at the head table. Why don't you drop your things and Phil can get you a drink?"

"Can I get you anything, Mom?" Phil asked.

"I'd love a glass of wine, honey, if you don't mind. I've just got to fuss with the centerpiece one more time before everyone gets here."

"You and Sheryl really outdid yourselves. Everything looks great."

She smiled up at her son. "Thanks, honey. You two enjoy yourselves. You make sure you introduce Margot around. I got lots of questions about your pretty girlfriend after last night's game."

She slipped away and made a mental note to ask the DJ to play lots of slow songs. She wanted to see her son and his girl on the dance floor later.

\*\*\*

"You didn't tell your mom we're not dating?" Margot asked.

Phil glanced around the room, from the decorated six foot tables to the bar in back corner of the room. He'd barely looked at her since she'd come down the stairs feeling awkward in the strapless dress and three inch platform pumps Kate had picked out for her to wear. She'd nearly stumbled when she'd seen Phil in the foyer wearing a suit as dark as his mood.

"No. I should have, but I didn't want to make her feel any worse about what she'd done."

If his mom thought they were still dating, there was no way they'd get out of sharing the bed that night. She'd barely been able to look at the bed after their afternoon spent watching the horses and their uncomfortable outing to the Dairy Barn.

They walked to the table where Margot left her purse and wrap and made their way to the bar. Phil introduced her to the man serving drinks before ordering a beer and two glasses of white wine. The room began to fill with people of all ages. Margot grabbed the wine glass like a lifeline and took a hearty gulp. She followed him around the room, from one set of folks to another. He'd introduce her, talk about the old times with his friends and acquaintances, and ignore her completely. Not once did he touch her or look her in the eye. When she couldn't stand it any longer, she excused herself, got another glass of wine from the bar, and sat down at their empty table where she could rest her feet and watch him from a distance.

Did he have to be the most handsome man in the room? With his height, she couldn't help but stare. Why wouldn't he look at her? Why did she get the feeling in his stony expression that she'd somehow made him mad? She felt relieved when Devon's wife Sheryl took the seat next to her and huffed out a loud breath.

"Lord have mercy, I'm tired. And this party's just getting started."

"Everything looks wonderful. You and Judy did a great job decorating."

Sheryl looked around. "It does look nice, if I do say so myself." She poured a glass of water from the table's pitcher and took a long sip. "Bo won't even notice, though. He hates to be the center of attention."

Margot spied Devon in a large group of men. All eyes were on him as he told some story with his hands flailing and his dimples shining. "Devon sure doesn't take after his dad in that regard."

Sheryl snorted. "Hell no, he doesn't. Wait 'til the music starts and he hits the dance floor."

Margot sat up straight when she saw Phil approach Julianne and her husband by the bar. "What do you know about Phil and Julianne?"

"They were hot and heavy in high school. Everybody thought they'd end up getting married, including Phil." She slipped off one of her shoes and rubbed her foot. "Shocked the whole town when Julianne broke up with him and not a month later started dating Stan. His mom about had a heart attack." Sheryl glanced over to the bar where the three of them stood talking. "Judy swears that's why Phil didn't come home after college and, truth be told, I think she's held a grudge ever since." She let out a sigh and rested her head on her palm. "Phil would have been miserable here. The two of you are a much better match than he and Julianne."

Margot couldn't let Sheryl's comment go without probing. "Why do you say that?"

"I don't know how to say it exactly, but she was too prissy for him. She was always telling him what to do and how to do it. He dodged the bullet with that one if you ask me."

Margot couldn't help but feel better at Sheryl's analysis of her and Phil. She agreed that she and Phil would make a perfect couple. If only he thought so, too.

***

Phil spied Margot sitting at the table with Sheryl and heaved a sigh of relief. He'd been heading in her direction, guilt ridden for having her sit alone in a crowded room, when Sheryl had saved him and sat down next to her. He felt like he was being torn in two. Half of him wanted to back her into the coat closet and fuck her brains out while the other half couldn't look at her for fear of not being able to tear his eyes away. He'd almost passed out when she'd walked down the stairs at his mother's house, her shapely calves showcased in three inch pumps and a cinnamon colored dress that hung just above her fabulous knees. The woman even had sexy knees.

She didn't have any better sense than to wear a sleeveless dress in October in Cash. With her hair pulled up and her neck exposed, he understood what if meant to yearn. He'd wanted to take a nip at the nape of her neck like the mating stallion and mount her on the stairs. Damn Devon and his offer to help.

"Huh?" Phil said when he realized Julianne had asked him a question and he'd been too enthralled with Margot to hear.

"When are you going back home?"

"Oh, tomorrow. Margot's got an exam to study for and I've got a lot of work to do."

"Margot's a college student?" Julianne asked with a touch of horror in her voice.

Phil's hackles were up in an instant. "She put herself through school. She's got to pass her licensing exam, and then she's a nurse."

Julianne must have detected the pride in his voice. His parents had paid for every bit of his education. He didn't know how far he would have gotten if he'd had to do it on his own.

"I'm happy for you, Phil. She seems like a lovely girl."

"She's twenty-five, Julianne. I'd hardly call her a girl." Yet hadn't he considered her a girl the whole time she'd worked for him? Hadn't he thought her too young?

"There you are," Devon said, interrupting Stan and pulling Phil out from the grips of his condemning ex. "So how'd it go this afternoon?"

"Fine," Phil said.

"Fine? Bet you didn't make it past the drive before she jumped you. Works every time."

Phil shoved his brother in the shoulder and away from the masses. "I don't need you butting your nose in my business, Dev."

"Holy shit. You're wound tighter than a drum. You still didn't bang her?"

Phil dragged Devon outside, past the awning and into the darkened parking lot. "We're not a couple," Phil admitted. "I brought Margot home just to get mom off my back and to quell the gay rumors."

Dev shook his head in disgust. "That girl's a sure thing. I think *I* could have fucked her after the breeding. What the hell are you waiting for?"

"She's dating a friend and a client. I can't go there with her." No matter how much he wanted to. No matter how much the desire to was eating him alive.

"Who gives a fuck, Phil? Is your friend in Cash? She's here, you're here. You obviously like her. Hell, she's smoking hot. I'd have mounted her before I ever hit the drive."

Phil shoved Devon into a late model sedan. "Shut the fuck up, you little pervert."

"I didn't say I would have, just that I could have. I'm a married man. You say what you want, but that little filly is hot for you. How tight can she be with her boyfriend if she's here with you? Go for it, man. Jesus, you're the only one of us who can. Quit being a pussy and ride the girl."

"You don't understand."

"You're right, I don't." Dev shrugged and straightened his tie. "Maybe those gay rumors aren't as off the mark as we thought."

\*\*\*

Margot felt hands on her shoulders and nearly died of delight when she realized Phil stood behind her.

"Let's dance," he said into her ear. He led her to the dance floor where couples swayed to the tune of a classic seventies ballad.

When Phil pulled her into his chest, Margot didn't know if her lightheadedness was from the wine or the feel of Phil's hand at her waist. If only he'd pull her closer and end the ache she'd felt since last night.

"You disappeared for a while," she said to break the silence. Despite his invitation to dance, he still wasn't looking her in the eye.

"Dev and I needed some air."

"Oh."

The music stopped and he let go of her and stepped back. "We'd better have a seat before dinner is served."

She felt disappointed that he didn't want to keep dancing as her favorite country song started playing over the loud speakers. "Okay."

"Excuse me," Dev said and reached his hand out for Margot. "How about a dance for your boyfriend's little brother?"

Margot looked at Phil, who glared at Devon with narrowed eyes. "Um, I guess," she said when Phil did nothing to stop them.

Devon whisked her into his arms and proceeded to lead her through an intricate series of dance steps that she struggled to follow. "Wow, Devon. You're quite the dancer," she said when he jerked her against his chest, and they swayed back and forth until the chorus started up and she knew he'd swing her back into action. She looked over his shoulder to see Phil standing at the edge of the dance floor, a scowl on his incredibly handsome face. He wasn't looking at her, but seemed to look through her. She caught her breath as Devon whisked her in a circle for another round.

"I'm cutting in," Phil announced. He pulled Margot from Devon's embrace and locked his arm around her waist, nearly lifting her off her toes. She could have moaned in delight. "Get your own woman." His hands came around her waist and she locked her arms around his neck. She'd never seen such a fierce look in his eyes. "You're not helping convince Cash we're a couple by dancing with my brother," he said.

"You might actually have to look at me to convince people we're together," she shot back.

As soon as their eyes met, as soon as she saw his jaw tighten and his pupils enlarge, she understood. He dipped his head and nestled his lips against the nape of her neck. "How about this?" He trailed his lips up to her ear and nipped at her lobe. "This helping at all?"

Margot grabbed his head and brought it down to hers, pulling his bottom lip between her teeth. Without warning, without anything to predict his reaction other than a predatory look in his eyes, he dove in. His hands were on her hips, lifting her off her toes, aligning their bodies for maximum friction. She heard the catcalls and snickers, but couldn't bring herself to care. Good Lord, the man could kiss. This wasn't like the slow buildup at the stadium where she felt herself slipping into the lolling waves on a calm clear day. This was like riding the cresting waves of a storm, like getting pulled under by the current and caught in the riptide.

When she started to moan, he caught her lips and swallowed the sound. He pulled back, his chest rising up and down with the effort. "Damn it, Margot. I don't want to take advantage of you like this."

Take advantage, please, she wanted to say. Use me. Abuse me. Do whatever you want with me. Please, just don't stop. "It's for show, Phil. You're not taking advantage." She dug her fingers into his scalp and brought his mouth to hers. "Do you want people to think you're gay?" she asked before devouring him.

*** 

The sound of silverware clinking on glass helped him regain a thin hold on sanity. One more minute, one more second, and he would have taken her on the parquet dance floor of his father's retirement party. "That should do it," he said through gritted teeth.

She stared up at him, her eyes huge and unfocused. This dinner couldn't end fast enough. He was either going to immerse himself in a tub of ice water or have her later that night. He had a pretty good feeling which way the pendulum swung when she bit her bottom lip and smiled up at him like the cat who'd swallowed an entire forest full of canaries.

It took an excruciating three courses, countless toasts, and a sweet solo dance for his parents to end the night. That alone was worth sitting through the evening with the smell of Margot's perfume enticing his over stimulated libido. And Margot, the vixen. She wiped crumbs from his shirt front with an erotic touch of her fingers. Her legs brushed his under the table, just enough to stir his juices. She licked the spoon while eating cheesecake as if stroking her tongue over him. He was going to have her tonight, damn the consequences, damn his parents in the next room, damn all common sense. He was too far gone to care.

# CHAPTER 17

His mom refused Margot's offer to help clean up.

"You kids have an early flight in the morning," she said. "Whatever we don't get to tonight, I'll drag your dad over here tomorrow. We'll have this knocked out before church."

She didn't have to go back to the table to get her wrap and purse. Phil had draped the wrap over her shoulders as soon as his mother began speaking and had shoved her purse in her arms before she'd finished. He kissed his mom on the cheek, gave his dad a handshake and a hug, and beat a hasty path to the door dragging Margot behind. She had to stutter-step to keep up. He either had to use the bathroom or he'd finally decided to quit fighting their attraction. She prayed it was the latter.

Once inside the car, she had her answer. He started the ignition, turned on the heat, and pulled her across the console for a mind-melting kiss. If they hadn't been in a crowded parking lot, she would have climbed over and ended it once and for all.

"Is this for show, too?" she asked, pulling back because the gearshift had damn near poked a hole in her abdomen.

He ran his hand through his hair and turned to look at her. "Do you want it to be?"

"I don't even know what you're asking," she said. Could he be more obtuse? She couldn't have been more obvious with her intentions if she'd written 'take me' on her forehead.

He heaved out a sigh. "I'm about at the end of my tether with you, Margot. There isn't a chance in hell I can sleep in that bed and not put my hands on you tonight. You've got to tell me and tell me now if I should sleep on the couch."

Good grief. After all this, he was going to make her say it? "I don't want you to sleep on the couch, Phil. I don't want you to sleep at all."

He slammed the car into gear and gunned the engine. "It's going to take about ten minutes to get home. You've got that long to change your mind."

Was he trying to talk her out of it? "I'm not going to change my mind. If you don't take me tonight, you're going to have to lay there and listen while I do things myself."

He groaned and stepped on the gas. "I think I can make it in less than ten." He gave her a mischievous grin. "What do you say we try?"

She reached over and put her hand on his thigh. His erection strained against his pants. "What do you say I give you a little motivation?"

"You've been motivating me for over twenty-four hours." He picked up her hand, bit her knuckles, and placed it back in her lap. "Any more and I might not make it."

"Then hurry. I'm at the end of my tether, too."

\*\*\*

He gunned it up the drive and slammed the car into park. He could barely get the keys out of the ignition with his hands trembling the way they did. When was the last time he'd trembled in anticipation of a woman? And yes, it was for Margot. Young, silly, snort-laughing, beautiful, sexy Margot.

She was halfway to the porch before he got out of the car. He caught up to her and picked her up off her feet, carrying her up the stairs to the door while her laughter rang out in his ears. He plunked her down and used the key to open the house. He kicked the door closed with his foot and backed her against it, his mouth on her neck, his hands on her breasts. He kissed up her jaw and tried to shift the strapless bodice down, but it wouldn't budge.

"Zipper," Margot moaned. "In the back."

He flung her around and began unzipping the dress while he pushed her toward the stairs. "Up, now, or I'm going to take you right here."

She jogged up, holding the dress in place with her hands. The parted chiffon revealed black thong panties and a bare back. He was so hard he could barely maneuver the stairs. When he made it to the landing, she stood at the threshold of the door wearing nothing but her thong and heels. If his groin didn't hurt so damn much, he would have thought he'd died and gone to heaven.

"Are you coming?" she asked as he gripped the newel post and looked his fill. She was magnificent. Her curls were popping free from her pins and hung around her face. The pale white of her skin was such a contrast to the hard pink tips of her nipples. The small tapered waist held up a daringly tiny swatch of underwear.

He met her in the doorway and took her breasts in his hands. "I think we both are. Very soon."

Her eyes fluttered closed. "Not too soon, I hope."

He backed her into the room and pushed the door closed with his elbow. He gripped her hips in his hands and lifted her against his erection while dipping his mouth to feast on her breast. She wrapped her legs around him and he lost his mind. "One of us is wearing too many clothes," she said.

He carried her to the bed and eased her down. "Yes, one of us is." He used his teeth to tear away her panties.

She gasped and tugged at his tie. "I want you naked," she said. "I want you on me, in me, please. Get out of these clothes."

He was hanging on by a thread. He wrestled with the buttons of his shirt while she pulled his tie free. He lifted the shirt over his head while she snaked her hands beneath his undershirt. He whipped it off and flung it across the room. When he stood up to undo his belt and pants, she leaned down to take off her shoes. "Leave the shoes," he said.

"Hurry, Phil," she pleaded as he toed off his Oxford Balmorals as his pants fell to floor. The boxers and socks were off in a flash. He stood before her, his erection all but clipping her in the chin. She reached out and touched it with her finger.

He swallowed a groan as they both went still. The front door opened and his parents came inside, their animated voices carrying through the house. He thought she'd change her mind. He thought she'd rush to cover herself, although he knew there wasn't a chance in hell his parents would open their door. She did neither, but shocked him by reclining on the bed in the most erotic pose he'd ever seen. He covered her body with his and the bed groaned with the movement.

"This fucking bed."

Margot arched against him and gathered the comforter in her hands. "The floor. Now."

They probably made as much noise getting on the floor as they would have if they'd stayed on the bed. Margot stood up, Phil gathered the quilt and blanket and tossed it on the hardwood, and lowered Margot to the makeshift bed. The scent of her drove him mad, the taste of her skin had him resisting the urge to bite and bite hard. She drew him toward her, arched up, and he took her with one long, hard push. There was a moment before he moved, before he could bring himself to move, when the sight of her face in the moonlight, eyes closed, lips parted, with just a hint of a smile on her face, had something flashing through him, something wild and reckless, something he'd never felt before. But then she lifted her hips and he started the dance, back and forth, deeper and deeper with every stroke until he couldn't think, couldn't breath, couldn't do anything but let the animal in him take over.

Her nails dug into his back, her legs locked around his waist, and the heels he'd insisted she leave on poked him in the ass. Margot pushed at his chest, pushed him onto his back, and took him inside her with a moan that was his name. He watched her delicate form move over him. Lost in her own pleasure, she destroyed him. Her hands flew to her head and, with one twist, her hair tumbled down her back. She came with a muffled cry, his name on her lips. He'd never seen anything so erotically beautiful as Margot losing herself in pleasure. She collapsed on top of him. He tossed her onto her back, reached down and pulled off her shoes, and plunged back in. He was going to set them both free as he let the lion inside of him roar.

***

Phil lay full out on top of her, dragging air in through battered lungs. Every inch of Margot's body felt alive, and she could have wept for the perfection of their coupling. Three years, she thought, three years of fanaticizing about the man hadn't even come close to the exquisite pleasure of having him. She ran her hand down the muscles of his back, down to his butt, and back again, memorizing the texture of his skin, the play of his muscles, the scent of the man she loved.

Never before had she given herself with such reckless abandon. Flashes of what she'd said, what she'd done, entered her mind and she pushed it away. There would be time to analyze and obsess, but she didn't want to waste time doing that now, not when he was still inside her, atop her, his breath evening out. He shifted to the side and propped up on his elbow, his hand caressing her still sensitized breast.

"My God," he said. "Wow. That was...wow."

"Yeah. Definitely wow."

She pulled her courage together and snuck a glance at his face. His expression looked serious, too serious for the moment.

"Are you okay?" he asked.

Okay? "Believe it or not, Phil, I've had sex before."

"I...I meant the floor. Your back."

"I'm fine." Or at least she would be if he'd hold her, if he'd tell her how much being together meant to him other than scratching an itch.

He pulled the quilt around her and cocooned them both. She wasn't going to be a chicken and turn away, wondering what it all meant. She shifted to face him, her hand resting against his chest. She could feel his heart pounding beneath her fingertips.

"I never meant for this to happen," he said. "This wasn't why I asked you here."

She brought her fingers to his lips and stopped the string of apologies before she ended up in tears. "I'm not sorry it happened. I wish you weren't sorry, either."

He blew out a breath and rolled over onto his back. "I should be sorry, I know I should be sorry, but I'm not."

"Then no apologies." She snuggled closer, tossing her leg over his and wrapping her arm around his chest. This would more than likely be the only time in her life she'd have the chance to be with him like this, and she wasn't going to waste it wishing she'd done more to entice him. "The party was nice. I think your dad had a good time."

Phil chuckled. "Yeah, he likes to pretend he doesn't like the attention, but he does." He wrapped his hand around her and began making small circles on her shoulder.

"You're lucky, Phil. Your parents are happy. You have a great foundation here."

"I know. I don't think I appreciate them enough."

"You should. Take it from me, flaws and all, there's no substitute for family."

His hand stilled on her arm. "What happened to your mom?"

"She died. I told you that."

"You didn't tell me how."

"She was born with a heart condition. She didn't realize she had it until I was born. She lived a lot longer than anyone expected her to."

"What about your dad?" he asked.

She deliberately kept her voice even. "I never knew him."

"Is he dead?"

Margot sighed. "I thought he was. For a long time, I was led to believe he was dead." And oh, how she wished she still believed in that fairy tale.

"So…do you know him?"

She knew him all right, but that wasn't what Phil had asked. "Nope. I never met the man who loved my mother."

He continued rubbing circles on her shoulder, making it hard for her to concentrate. "So what do you do on holidays? Thanksgiving and Christmas?"

"I have an aunt who lives in Sumter. I usually go there, but my cousin is getting married in Barbados over Thanksgiving, so I'll probably just work."

"Work on Thanksgiving?"

"It's just a meal, Phil. The double-time pay will go a long way toward paying back my loans." She glanced up when his hand tightened on her shoulder. He studied her with an intense expression on his face.

"What's wrong?" she asked.

"I don't like the thought of you being along on Thanksgiving."

"I won't be alone. I'll be surrounded by hundreds of people in the hospital."

"That's not the same."

"Maybe for you, but it seems like home to me." She reached her hand down and cupped his very fine ass in her palm. "That's why you're lucky, Phil. No matter where you live, you can always come home and know your family loves you." She pinched his butt in hopes of diverting his attention. "Even if you are gay."

He leaned up and pinned her hands above her head. "Gay, huh?" His lips brushed hers ever so lightly as he settled between her legs. "We'll just have to see about that."

# CHAPTER 18

Judy tiptoed down the hallway, past the bath where either Phil or Margot or maybe even both of them showered in the pre-dawn morning. She hadn't needed to set her alarm to get up and start the day. Bo's tossing and turning had left them both unable to sleep.

At least they weren't the only ones.

Coffee. She needed coffee and the monotonous task of making breakfast to steady her nerves after listening to her son and his girlfriend have sex all night long. She didn't know whether to feel proud or sickened that he had the stamina to keep going for hours. He certainly hadn't gotten that from his father.

She heard the bathroom door open and quickened her pace, unable and unwilling to face either of them before she'd composed herself. She set the coffee machine on brew and was just pulling the eggs from the refrigerator when Bo entered the kitchen wearing his Sunday finest, his hair still wet from the shower and a scowl etched on his face.

"You making that for me or the love birds?" he asked. "I'd imagine they worked up quite an appetite."

Judy sighed. "Get it out now, Bo, before they come down. I won't have you embarrass me before they leave."

"My comments would embarrass you? Really? Not the hours our son spent fornicating with his girlfriend right under our nose?"

"They're adults, Bo. He's not a child anymore."

"Lucky for him, or I'd have his butt in the field picking corn by hand for the next half century." He retrieved the milk from the refrigerator in anticipation of his coffee. "This is all your fault, you know."

She sighed and bit her tongue. She knew this was coming and, although she agreed with her husband, admitting she was to blame for the fornicating didn't sit well in her mind.

"Setting everything up so they'd have to sleep together," he mumbled. "Starting that stupid rumor. You may as well have ordered pornography on the television and suggested they watch a movie before bed."

"You finished yet?" she asked.

"It would help ease the sting if you'd just admit, for once in your life, that you were wrong."

"Alright!" She tossed the eggshells into the trash and slammed the cabinet door closed. "I was wrong. Are you happy now?"

"No. I'm not."

"I should have talked to him about his life, and if it makes you feel any better, he told me the same just yesterday. I don't think I'll have to resort to tricks anymore."

"Well, hallelujah," Bo said. "After what happened last night, that boy better put a ring on her finger if he knows what's good for him. At least when Devon nailed Sheryl, they were married."

"If you think Devon and Sheryl waited until they were married, you have a very selective memory."

"I didn't say they waited to have sex until they were married, I said they waited to have sex in our house until they were married."

Poor Bo, Judy thought. He really didn't have a clue.

Bo got a mug from the counter when the machine let out a blast of steam indicating the end of the brewing cycle. His hand jerked, spilling coffee on the counter when he heard footsteps on the stairs. "You do the talking," he told Judy. "I don't think I can even look that little girl in the eye."

Phil entered the kitchen, acting as if nothing out of the ordinary had happened the night before.

"Morning," Judy said with a quick smile over her shoulder. Bo didn't turn around from the counter.

"I hope you're not making that for us, Mom. Margot and I have to get going in just a minute if we want to catch our flight."

She turned around and raised her hands in the air. "What about breakfast?"

"Coffee's fine. We'll grab something quick along the way."

"Oh, Phil. I hate to send you off with an empty stomach."

He kissed her cheek and tried to squeeze next to his dad for a much-needed hit of caffeine. Bo edged away and made a beeline for the table. "We're fine, Mom. I promise. Do you have any to-go cups?"

Judy pointed to a cabinet above the fridge. Phil retrieved two Styrofoam cups from a sleeve and began filling them with coffee.

"Where's Margot?"

"She's almost ready. We've really got to hustle."

"I didn't realize how early you had to leave. I was hoping you could go to church and stay for lunch. I'm making your favorite roast."

"Ummm. I'll have to take a rain check." He took a sip of the piping hot coffee. "Do you still make it with the baby onions and carrots?"

"Just the way you like it." She turned the fire down on the stovetop and then reached up to cup his cheek in her palm. "I'll have to make it when you come for Thanksgiving. You're too skinny."

When he heard Margot struggling with her bag on the stairs, he turned on his heel and bolted from the room. Judy looked over at Bo, sitting at the table thumbing through the paper. "Aren't you going to get up and help them?"

"Why?" he asked. "Like you said, he's not a kid anymore."

She slapped him on the side of the head and carried the coffee Phil had made to the foyer. Margot looked too young to have spent the night sexing up her boy in her jeans, clogs, and t-shirt. At least the girl had the decency to look embarrassed, unlike Phil. So typical of men.

"Good morning, Margot." She handed the girl her coffee. "I hope you slept okay."

When she heard Bo snort from behind her, she felt relieved he'd joined them instead of her having to make a scene if he'd refused to say goodbye.

"Yes, ma'am. I can't thank you both enough for your hospitality."

"Oh, sweetheart, it was our pleasure."

"I think it was all hers," Bo whispered in her ear as Phil came back inside after carrying their suitcases to the car.

"You ready?" he asked his sex slave, er…, girlfriend.

She nodded and reached out to hug Judy. Thankfully she smelled like soap instead of Phil. Judy returned her embrace and watched nervously as she extended a hand to Bo. "Mr. Williams. Thank you, Sir."

He shook her hand and nodded, quickly looking away.

"Mom," Phil said with his arms outstretched for a hug. Her baby, her firstborn. She just couldn't stay mad. "I love you," he said.

She hated the way she fought tears every time he left. He and Bo exchanged handshakes before Phil and Margot disappeared out the door and down the drive.

"Oh, Bo. I wish he lived closer."

Bo shut the door in her face and gave her a mocking grin. "Don't worry, Jud. You can relive the good times while you're washing the sheets from their bedroom."

***

Phil entered the interstate toward St. Louis and glanced over to see Margot's head bobbing, her half-eaten breakfast sandwich in her lap.

He reached over and massaged her neck with his hand. "Go ahead and lean the seat back. Quit fighting sleep."

"No," she said. "I'm fine. I'm not going to sleep while you drive."

"Margot, you are sleeping. You can either be comfortable doing it or risk permanent neck damage. The choice is yours."

"You didn't get any more sleep than I did." She balled up her breakfast and tossed it into the bag. "I'm going to stay awake."

"Look, I've had so much coffee, there isn't a chance I'm going to nod off. Go ahead and lean back."

She shook her head.

"I'm just going to nag you until you do, so you may as well cooperate."

"Phil…"

"I'm fine. I'll sleep on the plane." He kept massaging her neck until her eyes drooped and, with a sigh, she let the seat back.

"Wake me up if you get tired."

"I will," he assured her.

"I'm just going to rest my eyes."

"Um huh." Thirty seconds later, she was gone. Her lips parted and every time he looked over, he could see a puddle of drool collecting in the corner of her mouth. The girl was exhausted.

She certainly had reason. Phil couldn't remember the last time he'd been up all night. Or most of the night. They'd collapse, doze, and then something would rouse him, a brush of her skin against his, the feel of her hair on his face, and he'd have to touch her, pull her closer, and as if on cue, their bodies would begin the dance again.

He kept waiting to feel guilty for sleeping with Margot, but so far he felt nothing but intense satisfaction, if not a little exhaustion. Even for him, last night had been a record. Strangely, the only guilt he felt this morning was that he'd disappointed his parents by having sex in their house. His father's behavior had certainly made it clear that he'd heard them. With Margot's penchant for moaning, it's not like he expected them to remain unaware. He couldn't wait to let her fly without restraint, although to say they showed restraint would be a stretch. She'd been, without a doubt, the most exciting lover he'd ever had.

She made a little noise in her sleep and he glanced over and smiled. How could she have been under his nose for three years and he knew so little about her? Her mother dead, her father completely out of the picture, and she planned to work on Thanksgiving to help pay back her loans. He'd dismissed her as a go-nowhere-in-life local with zero ambition. He'd never been so wrong about a person, except maybe Kelly Bristow.

He'd invite her to Thanksgiving with his parents, he decided as he exited the interstate toward the airport. He wouldn't let her spend the holiday alone.

# CHAPTER 19

Margot pulled out her study guide and notes before the plane took off, but didn't look at them until after the plane had leveled out in the sky. Phil had fallen asleep on her shoulder before the tires had even left the ground. She asked the flight attendant for a blanket and wedged it between her shoulder and his head to try and ease the stitch he'd surely have, but she wasn't sure how much the blanket helped.

He's so beautiful, she thought as she smoothed a lock of hair off his forehead. And good Lord, the man could move that mile-long body. She'd never been so thoroughly loved, from head to toe and back again. How would any man compare after Phil?

She sighed and tried to concentrate on her studies, but her mind was set on one thing alone: Phil. They hadn't spoken about a future, about what their night together meant, or where it might lead. She didn't want to spoil her memories with obsessive thoughts of what if when she could close her eyes and still feel him inside her. When she'd returned to the bedroom from showering, he'd pulled the towel away from her body and looked his fill with brown eyes as sweet and tempting as the caramel they reminded her of.

"I wanted to do this yesterday," he'd said with his clothes in his hand, ready to take his own shower. "And if we had more time…"

When he woke up, when they returned to South Carolina, would the sexual haze they were both under evaporate and leave her alone and shattered? Would they go their separate ways with a fond memory of their night together and the knowledge that his mission had been accomplished? The thought of not seeing him again, not having him again, left her bereft.

He muttered and twitched in his sleep, his knees jammed against the seat in front. The attendant knocked his elbow with the drink cart. He snuggled closer to Margot and flung his arm across her lap, atop her material. It was just as well, she thought with a sigh. She wasn't getting anything done, anyway. She leaned her head against his and tried to find some peace in sleep.

The landing woke her as she was jarred forward and her book slipped from out of her grip and fell to the floor. She reached down to gather the papers that had fallen with her book.

Phil jolted and blinked several times. "Wow," he said. "I don't even remember taking off."

Margot blew her hair out of her eyes. "You were out like a light."

"Boy, you're not kidding." He stretched and fidgeted in the seat while the plane taxied to the gate at Charleston's airport. "I feel better now, although I could eat a horse. Are you hungry?"

Her stomach growled at the mention of food.

"I'll take that as a yes," Phil said as he retrieved his cell phone from his bag and adjusted the settings. Margot watched his brow furrow. "I got a text from Danny. Kate's been admitted to the hospital. Pre-term labor."

Margot gasped. "Oh no." Her back pain. She should have known. "Does he say anything about what they're doing to stop it?"

"No. Just that she's at Charleston General."

"Call him, Phil. Find out the details if you can."

Margot stuffed her work into her carryon bag and listened as Phil spoke to Danny. She got frustratingly few details as Phil nodded his head and gave a few grunts of approval. He told Danny he'd call him later and not to worry about anything at the office. He clicked off his phone just as the seatbelt sign turned off and people began standing to collect their belongings.

"What'd he say?" Margot asked. "How is she?"

"She's resting now. They gave her some sort of drug to stop the labor."

"Probably terbutaline. That's the first line of defense." Margot nervously chewed her thumbnail. "I'm sure they started her on corticosteroids for the baby's lungs and some antibiotics."

"I think he said something like that. Margot?" He reached his hand out to still her nervous chomping. "Danny sounds scared."

"She's only…I don't know, thirty, thirty-one weeks. He has every right to be scared. I'll bet Kate's a mess."

"Is the baby going to make it?"

Margot shook her head. It was time to get a grip and not fill Phil's head with visions of the worst. "A lot of babies are born premature and are perfectly fine. Charleston General's got a great neo-natal wing. She couldn't be in better hands."

They gathered their things, exited the plane, and made their way silently to baggage claim. Margot couldn't stop thinking of everything that could go wrong for the baby. She needed to get to the hospital and check on her friend. Phil pulled her suitcase off the luggage carousel and retrieved his own.

"I want to go to the hospital," she said. "Can we go straight there?"

Phil stopped to take off the jacket he'd worn in Illinois. "Danny wanted me to bring him some stuff from the office. Do you mind if we run by there first?"

Margot felt a hand on her sleeve and turned around. She couldn't have been more surprised if Phil's mother had stood before her. "Randall?"

"Maggie, I've been calling your name. I guess you didn't hear me."

"What are you doing here?" she asked.

He looked at Phil. "Williams." And back to Margot. "Something going on here I should know about?"

Before she could answer, Phil stepped forward. "McBain. You trolling the airport now?"

"I just dropped off my sister." He put his hands in his pockets in what seemed like a casual move that was anything but when she saw him clench his jaw. "Where have you two been?"

"Just flew in from St. Louis," Phil said. "We ran into each other on the plane."

Margot turned her head and gaped at Phil. He wouldn't look at her.

"You know one another?" Randall asked.

"Margot used to work for us," he said in a funny voice. "She's moving up in the world."

"Margot?" Randall asked.

She couldn't believe it. Phil couldn't even bring himself to admit they'd spent the weekend together. All her fantasies about them having a future went up in flames before her eyes. He was ashamed to be seen with her. "Huh?" she said.

"Phil called you Margot."

"That's my name."

"Then why does everyone at the hospital call you Maggie?"

"Nurse Jankowski. She just doesn't listen."

"Say no more." Randall rocked back and forth on his heels while they all stood in uncomfortable silence. "Well, I've got to get to the hospital."

"Would you mind giving Margot a ride?" Phil asked. "Danny's wife's been admitted to the hospital and she wants to stop by and see her."

It was like a one-two punch, right to her heart. The bastard.

"Sure," Randall said. "I'd be happy to." He reached down and pulled the handle to Margot's suitcase out of her grasp. "Ready?"

Margot looked at Phil. He met her eyes briefly before pulling his phone from his pocket and fiddling with the keyboard. "Yeah," she said to Randall, but stared at Phil. "It's the best offer I've had all day."

***

Phil watched Randall escort Margot through the glass doors and clamped his jaw tight when he spied McBain slip his palm around her waist. Fucking McBain. Margot was McBain's nurse Maggie, the tasty morsel he planned to use for research!

He swallowed his jealousy and slowly made his way in their wake, careful not to get too close. Somehow, in the haze of sexual satisfaction, he'd forgotten about McBain. He'd poached a friend's girlfriend—and a client. He should feel ashamed of himself, but he couldn't feel anything other that a red-hot blaze of anger at the thought of that son of a bitch laying a finger on his Margot.

He stopped short when he realized what he'd thought. She wasn't his. She'd never been his. The only time she'd ever been any part of his is when she was his receptionist, and now she wasn't even that.

She'd looked hurt and angry, worse than when she'd overheard him talking about her to Danny. He felt like a scumbag. He'd taken her for granted for years, taken advantage of her in the worst possible way, and then dismissed her as if she meant nothing to him when in fact that wasn't true. But what did she mean to him? He rubbed the heel of his hand over his chest and shook his head. Now he needed to apologize to her and explain, but he didn't know how to explain when he didn't understand how he felt. He needed to get some food because he couldn't think straight on an empty stomach.

# CHAPTER 20

Margot ditched Randall in the lobby and heaved a sigh of relief when the elevator doors closed and she was finally alone. She needed to clear her head and get a grip on her emotions so she could be there for her friend.

She got Kate's room number from the nurse on duty and entered her room after knocking. Kate gave a weary smile and waved Margot inside.

"How are you feeling?" Margot asked.

Kate shrugged. A monitor beside the bed recorded the baby's steady heartbeat. "The contractions have slowed, but they haven't stopped completely. Dr. Warren said if they don't stop in the next twelve hours, they're going to put me on another drug that's shown more success in stopping preterm labor."

"Nifedipine?" Margot asked.

"That sounds about right." She gripped her baby at the base of her mound and rubbed her stomach with her other hand. "My head is spinning with all the medical jargon. I just want someone to tell me my baby's going to be all right."

"Dr. Warren is good. Very good. And the neo-natal wing is one of the best in the country. You're in good hands here, Kate."

"I know. I keep telling myself that, but I can't help but worry." She swept a tear from her cheek. "Oh, God, Margot, I'm scared."

Margot rushed to her bedside and reached for her hand. The woman Margot had envied for having everything stood to lose what was most important. "I know you are, but you have to stay positive. Lean on me and Danny and anyone else, but don't lose hope."

"I'm not. I'm sorry for dumping on you, but I'm trying not to get upset around Danny." She grabbed a tissue from the bedside table and blew her nose. "He's trying to be strong for me, but he's scared, Margot. I've never seen him scared before."

"You and the baby mean everything to him, Kate. I've never seen a man so completely devoted to his family."

She nodded and stared down at her lap for a long moment before looking Margot in the eye. "I wish we'd found out the sex of the baby. He or she is fighting for its life and I don't even know what to call it." She waved her hand around the room. "This makes it all so real. I want to call my baby by name, let it know that I love it, but that I *can* wait to meet it." She shook her head from side to side. "I hate calling it an it!"

Margot nodded. This, at least, she could do for her friend. "I'm sure it's in the file. If you ask the doctor, he'll tell you what the sex is."

"He will? I just have to ask? Are you sure they know?"

"Positive. If you've had an ultrasound, and I assume after all this you have, then it's in there."

"Oh." She bit her lip. "I have to talk to Danny first, make sure he's okay with it."

"Okay with what?" Danny asked. Margot turned around and saw her former boss in jeans and a wrinkled button-down carrying a cup of coffee in his hand. He looked like he hadn't slept in days.

Margot stood up. "I'll get out of your hair," she said. "Keep thinking positive thoughts," she whispered to Kate.

She gave Danny a hug. "Your baby's a fighter, Danny, and your doctor is one of the best."

He narrowed his eyes at her. "I'll walk you out," he said to Margot. He set his coffee down on the table and squeezed Kate's foot through the blanket. "Be right back."

In the hallway, he expelled a big breath and leaned against the wall. In the bright fluorescent lighting, Margot couldn't help but notice the worry in his tired eyes. The man was exhausted.

"I'm worried about Kate," he said without preamble. "The doctor has been great so far, but I think she's thinking the worst."

"She's just scared, Danny. This is scary. The baby books don't prepare you for stuff like this."

"I just don't understand how this could have happened. She's been taking really good care of herself."

"Has the doctor said anything about what may have caused this?"

"He said it could have been an infection, or any number of things. I'm so tired I can't remember half of what he said."

"Look," Margot reached up and touched his arm. "I know a couple of the nurses on this floor. I'll ask around and see if I can find out anything that I may be able to explain to you in plain English."

"I'd appreciate that, Margot. I'm not sure what else to do and I hate feeling helpless. I should be able to take care of my wife and the baby and there's nothing I can do."

"You're being a rock for her, Danny. She can get through anything, the two of you can get through anything, as long as you're together. And you can pray."

"I've done a lot of that," he said. "Trust me."

"Good." He could barely keep his eyes open. "Danny, you won't be able to help Kate or the baby if you're dead on your feet. Why don't you go home for a few hours, get some sleep, take a shower, and eat some food? I'll stay with Kate until you get back."

He rubbed his forehead. "I can't leave her, Margot."

"Listen, I'm sure you left the house in a rush. Go home, take a nap, get some stuff that might make Kate feel better—some socks or slippers, her makeup, a toothbrush. I promise I won't leave her side until you return."

"I can't ask you to stay."

"You're not asking. I'm offering. I've got all my study material in the nurses' lounge on the main floor. You go talk to Kate, tell her you're going home for awhile, and I'll be back in a jiffy."

He nodded. "I do need to see about Teddy. We dropped him at Ricky and Shannon's without anything—food, bowls, a leash, nothing. He's probably driving them crazy."

"Go, but don't spend all the time running errands. Sleep is what you need most." She thought of Ricky and Shannon Brewster. If ever there were people who could handle a dog, it was the parents of four young boys. "Ask Shannon if she wants me to take the dog. I've got a fenced back yard and I'm off for the next week to study."

"I will." He embraced her in a hug. She felt her face blush from the unusual gesture. "I can't thank you enough."

"You can thank me by getting some sleep."

***

Phil unlocked the office door and turned off the alarm. He smelled the familiar scent of the new carpet and the red currant reed diffuser on Margot's desk. He grimaced when he saw the empty surface of her desk and the photo of a cat Rebecca had placed in the corner.

The sandwich he'd devoured hadn't helped his mood or his mind. He still felt conflicted. He needed to apologize to Margot, that was the only thing he knew for certain.

He dropped his bag on his guest chair and took a seat behind his desk. He knew he should boot up his computer, go through his emails, and get a little work done while he was there. He needed to give Margot some time with Kate before he rushed to the hospital with the files Danny had requested. He didn't want to take the chance he'd run into her and force a confrontation he wasn't prepared for. He ran his hands through his hair and leaned back in the chair, blowing out a breath of air when a speckle of clarity broke through his addled brain.

When Margot left with McBain, he'd felt itchy and panicked and totally unsure of what to do—exactly the way he'd been expecting to feel for having slept with her. Never, not once, even now, did he feel the least bit unnerved about what happened between them. He could still see her, stretched out on the floor of the guest room, bathed in moonlight, her hair tumbled around her face, her lips swollen and turned up in a smile. God, she was so beautiful. How had he ever thought her plain?

The ache he felt in his heart wasn't because he'd taken advantage of her. It wasn't because he'd done something he shouldn't have done. It wasn't even because he'd have to see her again and pretend like nothing had happened between them. The ache in his heart was because he'd let her walk away with McBain without a fight. Because he'd have to pretend nothing had happened between them because that's the choice he'd made at the airport.

Would McBain fire him for stealing Margot? Would it matter? He'd only done a few preliminary sketches for the doctor's building. It wasn't like he'd be out a bunch of time. He'd even skipped his usual retainer since McBain was a friend. The bastard.

And was Margot actually dating him? He'd never asked, he'd only assumed they were dating after watching them kiss on the sidewalk. But what if that was all they'd ever done? Was he willing to let Margot go over something that could mean nothing to her?

Whoa. He sat upright and got up to pace, grabbing his ball from the floor where he'd left it. What was he thinking? A relationship? If he fought for Margot and won, was he prepared to start a relationship with her?

He stopped and let the idea of it swirl around his head.

"Huh," he said aloud when the idea didn't cause him to run screaming from the building. And why would it, he wondered. He liked her; he'd always liked her. He respected her; after learning of her past and of what she'd been through in order to achieve her goals, he couldn't help but respect her. He wanted her; there was no denying the attraction. "Huh," he said again. "I'll be damned."

"You talking to yourself again?" Danny asked from the doorway, jarring Phil out of his thoughts.

"Jesus, you scared me. What are you doing here? I thought you were at the hospital with Kate."

"I was. Margot's with her now. She insisted I go home and get some sleep."

"Then what are you doing here?" Phil asked. "I told you I would bring the stuff to you."

"I knew you'd screw it up."

Danny's words were said in jest without any bluster. His friend and business partner was exhausted. "How is she?"

"Kate? She's…" He leaned against the doorframe and rubbed his hands over his face. "She's trying hard to stay strong, but she's worried. Hell, I'm worried. We've been trucking along like nothing could ever go wrong and then BAM, out of nowhere she starts having contractions." He pulled his hands away from his face and balled them into fists at his side. "I can't stand to see her in the hospital. I can't let anything happen to her or the baby."

Phil dropped the ball and walked to stand in front of Danny. He put a hand on his shoulder and patted a few times before dropping his arm. "Sounds like it's out of your hands, Dan. Margot's right, you need some sleep."

"I know. I'm just going to grab the stuff I need and get out of here."

Phil trailed Danny to his office. "Is there anything I can do?"

"No. I don't know."

"What else has to be done?"

Danny gathered some files from a stack on his messy desk. It was probably a good thing Danny came in. Phil would have had a hell of a time locating the files he'd asked for. "I've got to get Teddy from Ricky and Shannon. Apparently he's been using the kids' stuffed animals as chew toys and he did a number on Shannon's flowerbed."

"What are you going to do with him?"

"Margot offered to watch him this week while she's off."

"Margot did?"

"Yeah, she said she's got a fenced yard. The dog is probably going nuts around all those kids and without Kate—he adores her."

"Look," Phil said as an idea popped into his head. "Why don't you go home and get some sleep? I can run over to Ricky's and get Teddy."

Danny's head jerked up in surprise. "In your Mercedes?"

"Hell no, not in my Mercedes. I'll take the work truck."

Danny rubbed his temple. "I appreciate the offer, Phil, but I've still got to go home and get his stuff."

"What stuff?"

"His dog bed, his leash, his food."

Phil shrugged. "I can buy all that at the pet store. There's one on the way."

"Are you sure?" Danny asked.

"Would I offer if I wasn't?"

Danny put his hands on his hips and dropped his head. Phil feared his friend was on the edge of a breakdown. "Everybody's being so great. I just wish there was something I could do…"

"There is," Phil said. "Go get some rest. Kate needs you strong, bud. We'll handle the rest."

Danny nodded, picked up the files, and walked out the door. "Thanks, man."

"No problem. Tell Kate I'll be in to see her soon." As soon as Danny was gone, Phil retrieved the truck's keys from Margot's desk. "Okay," he said to himself. "Let's go get my excuse to see Margot."

# CHAPTER 21

When the doorbell rang at seven-thirty Sunday night, Margot looked down at her Snoopy pajamas and cringed. Why, on a night when she planned to go to bed as soon as the sun went down, did someone have to stop by?

She set her cookie on the coffee table next to her mug of tea and tiptoed to the door. She stretched on her tippy toes and peeked through the beveled glass window at the top of the door. Phil's shiny dark hair gleamed in her porch light. Oh no.

"What do you want?" she shouted through the wood.

"I've got something for you," Phil said.

"I'm busy. Just slide it under the door."

"It won't fit under the door. C'mon, Margot. Open up."

"Just leave it on the porch, then. I'll get it later." No way was she going to let him see her and Snoopy. Or anyone else.

His answer was drowned out by a booming bark. "What is that?" she asked.

"It's Teddy. Danny said you'd watch him."

Margot leaned against the door. "Let him out in the back. There's a gate to your left."

She felt the knock at her back like stakes to her bruised and battered heart. "He comes with accessories, Margot. You're going to have to open up. And if you care at all about these pansies you've got on the porch, you'll do it now."

She jerked the door open and gaped at the massive black and white dog with a petal in his mouth. "Bad dog," she said and shooed him away from the pot with her arms. When she looked up at Phil, he had a stupid grin on his face. Did the idiot have to look more handsome than ever?

"Snoopy, huh? Nice."

She yanked the leash from his hand. "Thanks, I can take it from here."

Teddy followed her into the house. She unhooked the leash and watched as he made a beeline for her cookie. She hopped around him and managed to stop her mug from overturning as he grabbed the cookie. "I guess he overstayed his welcome at the Brewster's?"

"They were more than happy to see him go." Phil stepped inside, closed the door, and looked around. At least he had the decency to look uncomfortable after dumping her on Randall at the airport. "You studying?"

"Trying to," she said. When Teddy took off down the hall toward her bedroom, she chased after him, closing doors as she went. She cornered him in her bathroom, grabbed his collar, and shooed him outside through her door to the patio. When she turned around, Phil was standing in her bedroom, looking bigger and more masculine than ever in her pretty master suite. The knowing look in his eye told her he'd like to use the bed that stood between them in the very near future.

"Your room smells like you."

She couldn't stand in her own home and be seduced by the man who'd dropped her like a hotcake as soon as the opportunity presented itself. She wouldn't allow herself to get burned by him again. Hadn't she spent all afternoon with Kate, relaying the details of the weekend, strengthening her resolve to forget what happened and move on?

"I've got a lot of work to do, Phil, and I'm tired."

"I know," he said, but made no attempt to leave. He stuffed his hands in the back pockets of his jeans and continued to stare at her.

Here it comes, she thought. The apology. The *I'm sorry I took advantage of you* speech. The *let's just be friends* number she'd steeled herself all day to hear. She wouldn't give him the satisfaction of saying it first.

"Look," she said. "Don't get all weird on me, okay? We had a good time, we scratched an itch, and now we're home. I'm not going to get all psycho on you, Phil. You don't have to stand here and try to dance around what happened. We're both adults, we shared a mutually satisfying experience, and now its over. I'm fine with it and it's only going to piss me off if you apologize."

He raised his brows and opened his mouth, but nothing came out. "Okay…" he finally managed after clearing his throat. "Is this because of McBain?"

Was it because of Randall? Of course it was because of Randall! He couldn't have dumped her on the good doctor any faster! "No, of course not. He needed to get to the hospital and so did I. You simply suggested that we ride together. Efficient as always."

"No, that's not—"

A yelping howl sounded from the backyard. Margot flicked on the porch light and dashed out the door, Phil on her heels. "Where is he?" she asked.

"I don't see him," Phil said.

Teddy gave another howl that led Margot and Phil to the corner of her half-acre lot where he'd wedged himself between a hole she hadn't known she had in her fence and had gotten stuck. His head was in the neighbor's yard while his body remained in hers. "Oh no. How are we going to get him out?"

Phil hopped over the fence in one impressive leap and began soothing the dog. "I'll push the fence apart while you pull his head back through. On the count of three. Ready?" he asked.

Margot nodded and they both counted aloud. Phil yanked the fence apart and Margot wedged his head back through. Teddy gave a whole body shake, what sounded like a thank you bark, and began dashing around the yard like a mad-dog.

Phil jumped back over and put his hands on his hips. "Do you have any wire or twine? If we don't close that gap, he's liable to get stuck again. I don't think he's the smartest dog on the planet."

"I'm sure there's something in the garage," Margot said. "I'll go get it."

When she came back with a few scraps of nylon string, she found Phil tossing a tennis ball to Teddy. "Where'd you get the ball?"

"Pet store," he said. "Danny said he'd retrieve until your arm falls off."

Margot watched Teddy race after the ball and return it to Phil's feet every time, eagerly waiting for the next toss. "Let's hope it wears him out." She handed him the twine and took his place throwing balls to Teddy. By the time Phil took over throwing the ball, Margot's arm ached. "I'm going to be sore tomorrow."

"You've got a pretty good arm," Phil said. "For a girl."

"I am a girl."

Phil threw the ball into a tangle of trees along the fence line where Margot knew Teddy wouldn't find it for awhile, especially in the dark. He turned to face her. "Yes," he said. "You are most definitely a girl."

Uh-oh. A deaf man would have recognized the meaning of his words. She wasn't doing this again. "Thanks for fixing the fence."

Teddy ran back with the ball between his teeth. She plied it loose and held tight. "It's getting late. You should probably go."

She couldn't see his face and had no way of knowing what he thought in the pause that followed. But she did see a shadow move in her house and the fall of a curtain from the back bedroom. She had to get Phil to leave. Fast.

She turned her back to him and walked to the gate, scanning the house as she went. He followed her to the driveway and to the tailgate of the Flannery & Williams truck. "Thanks for bringing him over," she said.

He pulled the food and a dog bed from the truck bed. "I'll carry these inside."

"No!" She stopped him by placing her hands on his chest. "Just put them on the porch. I'll bring them in later."

In the glow from the porch light, she could see his eyes narrow. "Don't be ridiculous," he said and pushed past her. "This bag weighs forty pounds." She quickly grabbed the other bags from the back and followed him to where he dropped Teddy's things in the foyer where she'd instructed him to leave them.

"Thanks again," she said with her hand on the open door. She couldn't wait for him to leave.

He stared down at her with a scowl on his face. "He's pretty strong. Make sure you keep a tight grip on his leash. Danny said he behaves best when he gets lots of exercise."

Why wouldn't he just go? Didn't he know that every second he stayed in her house was torture? "There are plenty of squirrels to chase in the backyard and I can take him down to the beach and wear him out."

"Margot," Phil reached his hand out to stop her from closing the door in his face. "I want to talk to you. About what happened," he said when she stared at him blankly.

She closed her eyes, more weary than she'd ever been in her life. "There's nothing to talk about, Phil."

"You don't think we should talk about it?" he asked.

"You don't have anything to feel guilty about, Phil. I absolve you."

"I'm not looking for absolution." He stuffed his hands in his pockets. "I'm not sure what I'm looking for, but I don't feel guilty."

Well, she thought. There you have it. Of course he didn't feel guilty. Hadn't she heard about his love 'em and leave 'em reputation for years? This was his MO. "Good. Neither do I, okay? I'm embarrassed, certainly, that your parents heard us, but I'm never going to see them again." She shrugged, becoming more and more uncomfortable as he stood unmoving in her doorway. "It's been a long day."

"Margot—" he started and then raised his brows when the old pipes moaned. The sound of a toilet flushing echoed through her small house.

Phil nodded his head knowingly and Margot couldn't look him in the eye. Let him assume the worst. The truth was so much harder to explain.

"There's someone here," he said.

"Yes." She snuck a glance and saw the cold speculation in his eyes.

"I see. You should have said so before and I wouldn't have bothered you." He backed out of the house and down the steps. "Good luck on your test."

Margot swallowed the lump in her throat and closed the door on any chance she had with the man she'd probably never get over.

"Who was that?" Ashley asked as she emerged from the hallway wearing flannel pants and an oversized sweatshirt.

"Phil." Margot opened the back door and let Teddy inside. He bounded up to Ashley and sniffed her crotch.

"Uh," she cried. "What is this?"

"His name's Teddy. He's a house guest, like you, except he was invited."

She sneered at Margot. "Very funny. I'm not a house guest," she corrected. "I'm family."

Margot looked at her half-sister. They looked nothing alike. With Ashley's straight brown hair and aristocratic features, no one would ever have guessed they were related.

"Only when it's convenient."

"What is that supposed to mean?" Ashley asked with her trademark pout. The best thing for everyone, her father included, was if Margot had turned her away instead of letting her stay when they'd kicked her out.

"You need to go home and face them, Ash. You can't hide out here forever."

"You don't understand," Ashley muttered. "You've never lived with Dad. He's a tyrant."

Of course she'd never lived with their father. Until a few years ago, she hadn't known he'd existed. And since that time, she'd seen more of her sister than any other member of her 'family.' "They weren't being that unreasonable," Margot said. "You are twenty-three years old. I don't think you should be shocked that they asked you to cook a meal every now and again or pick up after yourself. I certainly won't cook your meals or let you turn my house into a pigsty."

"But I'm their daughter," she wailed. "And that's my house. You don't have to pick up after yourself in your own house if you don't want to."

Margot was too emotionally spent for Ashley's drama. If she thought she could trust her, Margot would have told her what real drama was like. "Of course I do," she said. Her head was beginning to pound and she wanted nothing more than to go to bed. "I certainly can't afford a maid."

"Uh," Ashley said, and threw her body onto the couch. Teddy walked over and laid his head in her lap. "You sound just like mom."

"Well, I'm not your mother." Margot picked up Teddy's dog bed. "You have a college degree in accounting and you work at The Coffee Bean. Frankly, I can understand why they're upset with you."

Ashley sat up and wrapped her arms around her up drawn knees. "I don't want to be an accountant," she whined. "It's so boring."

"Then why did you major in accounting?" Margot asked.

"Because I'm good at math and Dad kept saying I should concentrate on what I'm good at."

Margot bit her tongue. There wasn't any use in getting between her father and his wayward daughter. Just because Margot had scrimped and sweated and clawed her way through school on her own dime didn't give her the right to call Ashley selfish because she'd been spoon fed everything she ever wanted from the time she was born. "Ash, you're wasting your education. Your degree can open up so many doors for you. I'm sure they're just upset that you're not even trying."

"I have tried, Margot. I have. But I like working at The Coffee Bean. The people there are so nice."

Margot rubbed her head. "There are nice people everywhere. You just need to find the right company. Something small." She grabbed Teddy by the collar. "I'll pick up a paper tomorrow and we can go through the ads together."

"Margot?" Ashley called. "Thanks. I don't know what I ever did without you."

# CHAPTER 22

Phil sat at his desk and couldn't concentrate. It had been four days since he'd seen Margot and his insides were shot to hell. He ran for miles every morning trying to cure his sleeplessness, but his runs only left him drained of energy and starving. He didn't go to the club for fear he'd run into McBain and say or do something he'd regret. And at the office, the one place he'd always been able to feel comfortable, he couldn't relax because nothing felt the same.

Damn Margot for changing everything about his life! A knock at his door brought him out of his thoughts.

Rebecca stood at the threshold in a crisply starched shirt and pants. Her hair was neatly pinned in a professional bun. He couldn't stand the way she never had a hair out of place. "Excuse me," she said in her irritating voice. "Randall McBain called again when you were at lunch. He wants to meet about his plans as soon as possible."

Of course he did. He couldn't avoid the man forever. "I'll call him, Rebecca. Thanks."

When she didn't move, he looked up again to see the bag he'd left on her desk in her hand. "I appreciate these treats you keep bringing, but...to be honest, I don't particularly care for sweets." She walked over and placed the bag of cookies on his desk.

Phil watched her walk out and reached inside the bag for an oatmeal raisin cookie—Margot's favorite. He took a bite and slammed his fist on the desk. That was the last straw. He got up and shut the door, picked up the phone, dialed Margot's home

Christy Hayes

number from memory, and waited until she answered on the third ring.

"Hello?"

The sound of her voice had his muscles clenching. "I need you to come back," he said without preamble. "Rebecca isn't going to work out. She's terrible."

Margot huffed out a breath. "Well, hello to you, too."

"Sorry, but I can't take it any more."

"What's the problem? I told her she could call me if she had any questions and she hasn't called once. I assumed everything was going fine."

"Well, you assumed wrong. She comes into my office every morning and arranges the files on my desk according to my appointment schedule."

"That sounds wonderfully efficient."

"Yes, it would be if I didn't hate it when someone messed with my stuff."

"Okay," she said as if speaking to a toddler. Phil didn't appreciate her tone one bit. "Did you explain to her that you don't want her messing with your office?"

"What good would that do?" he asked. "She's already been banned from Danny's office. If I tell her to stay out of mine, she'll quit for sure." Then Margot would have to come back. "Maybe I should tell her to stay out."

"You can't tell her to stay out completely. Just calm down. I'll call her and explain that you only like certain things touched. Will that make everything better?"

"No. That's just the tip of the iceberg." He tapped his fingers on the desk. "She talks so loud, Margot. I can hear her even when my door is shut."

"You never shut your door," she said.

"I do now. And her voice. I told you her voice gets on my nerves."

"There's nothing I can do about her voice, Phil."

"And she doesn't like sweets!" He took another bite of the Island's best cookies. "I brought her cookies from Misa's bakery and she returned them. She said she doesn't care for sweets.

Who doesn't care for sweets? There's something wrong with her."

Margot sighed again, getting his hackled up. "I'll call her about the office bit, but the rest is all about you."

"It's not about me, Margot, it's about her. I don't like her."

"You didn't like me and we got along just fine."

He felt like he'd been slapped. "What do you mean I didn't like you? Of course I liked you. I still like you." *I'm falling apart because I don't see you everyday*, he wanted to say, but bit his tongue and said the only thing that was true. "I want you back, Margot."

"I can't come back, Phil. Think about what you're asking."

He knew what he was asking. If only she knew exactly what he was asking. "It's not the same. Nothing is the same anymore and I hate it."

"You're just going through an adjustment period right now. Give it a week or two and you'll feel much better. I promise you will."

"How can you be so sure?" he asked. She'd settled him down enough to realize he missed her dreadfully. If he couldn't have her in his personal like, he wanted her in his life however he could have her.

"Because I know you. You don't like change. Give it a couple of weeks and it won't feel so different. You might even learn to like Rebecca. You learned to like me."

He was afraid his feelings had gone way beyond like where Margot was concerned. "You were easy to like. You still are."

"Are you better now?" she asked.

"I guess."

"Good. My test is tomorrow and it's crunch time. I've really got to go."

He sighed. "Haven't you had all week to study?"

"Yes, but there have been too many distractions. I can see the finish line and I'm getting nervous."

By distractions, she meant McBain. His hand tightened on the receiver. "You'll do fine, Margot. Besides, if you don't know it by now, you never will."

"Thanks for the confidence boost," she said.

"That's not what I meant. Look, you're one of the smartest people I know."

"You wouldn't have said that a week ago."

The fact that she was right only made him feel worse. "And I would have been wrong. Trust me, you're going to pass."

"I hope so."

In the pause, he could hear her breath through the phone. He wanted so badly to go over to her house and become her number one distraction. "I'd better let you go."

"Yeah," she said. "You probably should. Bye, Phil."

"Bye." He hung up and rubbed his hand over his chest where it ached. Damn it all to hell. He more than liked her. He was in love with her.

***

Margot set the phone on the coffee table, leaned back against the couch, and closed her eyes. Why, why, why did he have to stir her up like he did? And why now? Her test was tomorrow and her head was spinning with formulas, calculations, and protocols. Not to mention all the obsessive thoughts she had about Phil.

Teddy got up from the floor and stood before her, putting his head in her lap. The dog had become increasingly sensitive to her moods. "I know," she cooed and rubbed his head. "We're both a little bit heart broken, big guy. The difference is," she explained when he gave a groan of pleasure as she began scratching behind his ears, "you get to go back to the ones you love. I, on the other hand, will end up alone, as usual."

*I want you back*, she heard his words echo in her heart. I want you back, too, she thought. Oh, how she wanted him back.

Ashley came in through the side door, causing Teddy to let out a startling bark.

"It's just me," she called from the kitchen. "I've got muffins."

Margot got stale muffins from The Coffee Bean and Rebecca had turned away Phil's cookies from Misa's. She reminded herself that nursing was what she wanted as she stacked her study materials in a pile and shuffled into the kitchen.

"What kind?" she asked Ashley.

Her sister had filled the kettle and turned the stove on to heat water for tea. "Some kind of pumpkin concoction that didn't sell very well. They're not bad."

Margot sniffed, shrugged, and set a muffin on a plate. "Want one?"

"No, I'm just going to have some tea. It's really gotten chilly outside."

Margot looked through the window to the darkening clouds. "It looks like rain." The gray sky matched her mood perfectly.

"What's wrong with you?" Ashley asked. "Are you worried about your test?"

"No. I don't think I can study any more."

"Then why do you look like you've lost your best friend?"

Because she had. As miserable as she felt after hanging up the phone with Phil, listening to him whine about Rebecca and all the ways his life had changed had been the best few minutes of her week. "I'm just anxious to get on with the next stage of my life, that's all." She sat down at her kitchen table. "Speaking of which, did you follow up on any of those ads?"

Ashley turned from the counter to face Margot with a beaming smile. "As a matter of fact, I did. I've got an interview tomorrow with a flower shop in Andover. They're looking for a bookkeeper."

"Is it fulltime or part-time?" Margot asked. She couldn't imagine a flower shop needing a fulltime bookkeeper.

"Part-time," Ashley answered with her eyes averted. "I figured that way I could still do some hours at The Coffee Bean."

"I thought we talked about this, Ash. You won't get any benefits from a part-time position."

"I know, but I'm still on Mom and Dad's insurance for a few more years."

"I thought you wanted to be independent? Go out on your own? How can you do that if they're paying for your insurance?"

"It's just an interview, Margot." Ashley began filling the mugs with water after the kettle started to sing. "Really, you're getting worked up over nothing."

"I just don't want you settling for less when you're capable of so much more."

"I'm not going to settle. I like to think of it as taking baby steps."

"As long as you're taking baby steps toward something with insurance and benefits," Margot said.

Ashley turned around. "Stop with the lectures. I know what I'm doing. Jeez, you're worse than my parents."

"Then why don't you go home?"

Ashley brought a mug of tea to the table. "It's bad enough listening to them harp at me about wasting my life. I swear, Margot, if you heard the things they said about you, you probably wouldn't take their side so much."

Margot swallowed a bite of muffin that had turned to paste in her mouth. She knew she shouldn't ask, it would only lead to more heartache and she didn't think she could handle any more. But she was never one to do what was best for her. Her weekend with Phil was evidence of that. "What are they saying?"

"Oh, the usual," Ashley said as if every word weren't tearing away bits of Margot's flesh. "That you're a bad influence, that I'm going to end up working at a menial job, having affairs with married men the way your mom did."

Margot washed away her bitter retort with a scalding sip of tea. "I'm sure they're just worried about you."

"And about me spending time with you. If they only knew you lectured me daily about the same things they try to lecture me about."

"Why don't you tell them?" Margot asked.

"And spoil the illusion that you're corrupting me with your wild ways? Never. It's too much fun knowing they think the worst."

Margot tossed her muffin in the trash and dumped her tea in the sink. "You know, Ashley, you're too old to play games with people's lives. You need to grow up."

Ashley pouted, cradling the cup of tea in her hands. "I don't understand why you defend them when they constantly say bad things about you. Can't you for once take my side?"

"They say bad things about me because they don't know me. You do, and you don't defend me. After everything I've tried to do for you, I don't appreciate being your scapegoat."

"Scapegoat? They're yelling at me, not at you. I'm actually protecting you from their wrath."

Margot shook her head and sighed. The girl would never learn. "Their wrath is called love, Ashley. They love you and they're concerned for your future. If you want to work part-time jobs and flitter around the rest of your life, fine by me. But do me a favor and have the guts to stand up and take responsibility for your decisions instead of letting me take the blame."

"I don't know what crawled up your butt," Ashley said with an annoying roll of her eyes. "But whatever it is, I sure hope it passes soon."

"Real life is what's crawled up my butt. Reality isn't one of your stupid TV shows. I'm responsible for myself because I don't have anyone to love me or to care what I do and how I live my life. So instead of pushing your parents away, you may want to thank them for caring so damn much and stop feeling sorry for yourself."

She turned on her heel and stormed to her room, Teddy in her wake. At least she had the dog, but even he was only a temporary visitor in her life. She threw herself atop her bed and did something she hadn't done in years. She curled up with her pillow and cried into the soft fabric to muffle the sound.

# CHAPTER 23

When Danny walked into the office, Phil felt relieved to break the tension between him and Rebecca. The girl hated him, Phil knew, and he didn't like the way she watched his every move. Phil followed Danny into his office and shut the door.

"What's up?" Danny asked. He pushed through the files on his desk in search of something specific.

"How's Kate?"

Danny stopped his search and leaned back in his chair. "She's better. The contractions have stopped and we thought they were going to let us out, but her blood pressure's too high." He rubbed his hands over his face. "I feel like we're going to be there until she delivers."

"That sucks for both of you," Phil said. "But it sounds like what's best for the baby."

"I know. Every time I start feeling sorry for us, I try to remember that we're lucky to have such a good hospital in our backyard."

"Sounds like the best you can do." Phil took a seat, flipping his ball between his hands. Danny pulled a piece of paper from his pocket and crossed a few items off his hand-written list before glancing up at Phil.

"What's wrong with you?" he asked.

"Nothing," Phil said.

"Nothing? You've got so little to do that you're just going to sit here and watch me? Must be nice," he muttered.

"All right, maybe it's not nothing. But it's not as big or important as having your wife in the hospital."

Danny sat back again and gave Phil his full attention. "Spill it. I've got some work to do before I head back."

Phil stood up and decided confiding in Danny was a bad idea. The man never had time for office gossip anyway. Wasn't that what he missed most about Margot? "Nevermind."

"No. You want to talk about something, so talk. I know you, you've got something on your mind."

Phil pursed his lips and then gave in. He sat back down when he realized he didn't have anyone else to talk to. "It's about Margot."

"What about Margot?"

"I…well, you know she went home with me over the weekend."

"Yeah."

"Well, we…I mean, things happened." He ducked his head and rubbed his neck before looking back up at Danny's impatient stare. "We slept together."

Danny blew out a breath. "I'm glad she doesn't work for us anymore."

"You're the only one," Phil muttered.

"What do you mean by that?"

"I'm just not crazy about Rebecca. She's so…formal."

"Isn't that what you were looking for in a receptionist? Someone to put a professional face on the front desk?"

"Well, yes, but, she's…" How could Phil explain to Danny how he just couldn't stand to see her—or anyone—in Margot's job? "She's cold."

"Cold?" Danny asked. "Sounds to me like you're missing Margot."

"Of course I miss Margot. Things ran smoothly when she was here."

"I know I've been out of the loop, but are you saying things aren't running smoothly with Rebecca? 'Cause she's been pretty great considering my situation with Kate."

"Okay, fine," Phil admitted. "She's doing a perfectly acceptable job."

"But?"

"But nothing. Never mind."

Danny started rocking back and forth in his seat, watching Phil with mild interest. "So since Rebecca is doing a perfectly acceptable job, this has to be about you and Margot."

Phil stared at his friend and business partner. The man with whom he'd turned a dream into reality. The man who'd lost his heart years ago and had never looked back. "She's dating McBain."

"Randall McBain? The plastic surgeon?"

"The one and only."

"So what?" Danny said. "I'd say if she slept with you, they're not exclusive."

"Yeah, I know. I mean, I hate poaching from a friend, but he's not exactly my favorite person. Not to mention the fact that he treats women like pieces of gum. As a matter of fact, I don't understand what Margot sees in him, except that he's a doctor and she's a nurse, so they have that medical connection."

"So go for it," Danny said and began flipping through some invoices.

Phil leaned over and stilled the papers. "There's just one problem." When Danny looked up, Phil said, "He's a client."

Danny nodded and reclined into the chair. "Ooh," he said. "I forgot about that." He lifted his brows. "That's a problem."

"I know. But the thing is, I'm not a hundred percent certain they're dating."

"Sounds like you're fishing for an excuse to sleep with her again."

Phil hopped up to pace, flipping his ball between his hands. "I know why you'd think that. I'm not exactly known as Mr. Relationship, but the thing is—and this is totally out of the blue—but I think I've got feelings for her. No, wait. I'm not going to lie. I've definitely got feelings for her."

"So you've got feelings for Margot and you think she's dating McBain. Why do you think they're dating? Did she admit it?"

"No. I saw them, right before we left, I saw them kissing on the sidewalk in Andover."

"Multiple kisses or just one?"

Phil thought back to that night on the street. He remembered the way Randall held her face in his palms, the startled look on Margot's face, the way she seemed to melt into the kiss that lasted too long to be considered chaste. "Just one, but it wasn't exactly short."

"Tongue?"

"I don't know. It was just a long, lingering kiss."

"So one kiss?" Danny asked. "What else?"

"He was at the airport when we landed."

"To pick her up?"

"I'm not sure. He said something about dropping his sister off and Margot seemed pretty surprised to see him, but you know what a weasel he can be."

"Doesn't sound like much, Phil. Sounds like the path is clear."

"There's more," Phil said. "I was at her house the other night, dropping off Teddy. Someone was there."

"Was it McBain?"

"I don't know for sure, but I'd bet it was him."

"Did you see his car?"

It had been dark when Phil had pulled into the driveway, but Margot's garage was behind her house. "No, but it could have been parked in the back."

"I don't know what to tell you, man. She's never admitted she's dating him and you've witnessed one kiss? I say screw McBain. One date doesn't equal dating."

"But what if they are?"

"Find out for sure and then make your move. Either way, I'm done talking about this. But if he's on the books, do us both a favor and don't do anything to screw it up."

"Yeah," Phil agreed. "Thanks for listening."

Under normal circumstances, he would have taken Danny's screw McBain advice and gone full steam ahead. As a matter of fact, he wouldn't have needed any advice. But this was Margot. This was different. This was important. He needed to think about his next move.

\*\*\*

Margot stretched her back after exiting the windowless room and decided to take the stairs instead of the elevator after sitting for so long. She felt invigorated since turning in her test. She'd passed. She knew it. All she needed now was to wait an excruciating forty-eight hours to have the results confirmed.

Finally things were coming together. She'd be on staff at the hospital by next week. Her new and improved life would begin in a matter of days. With the sun shining in the cloudless sky and her test behind her, why didn't she feel more optimistic?

She'd buried herself in her studies, pausing only long enough to take care of Teddy and listen to Ashley whine about how bad her life was. Uh. Margot couldn't bear to go straight home. She pulled off the interstate and decided to treat herself to something special. She drove into Charleston proper and pulled alongside the Inn boasting Charleston's legendary coconut cake. Margot was a sucker for coconut cake. In jeans and a button down, she wasn't anywhere near dressed for the restaurant, but she could place a takeout order and enjoy the lobby of the historic hotel while she waited.

She was sitting at the bar and sipping on a glass of water when she heard a booming laugh and footsteps on the patio's brick floor. She turned around in time to see her father's smile turn to a frown as he spotted her. She whipped around in her seat and willed him not to have recognized her.

"Well," he said. In just that one syllable, Margot recognized his disdain. "It's a little early for a cocktail."

She swiveled in her seat and looked him squarely in the eye. His companion had continued walking toward the hotel and the bartender had disappeared. She didn't want to be alone with Judge Hennessey. "I'd hardly call water a cocktail."

He snorted his disbelief and set his hand on the back of her chair, not allowing her to turn away at will. "What are you doing here? Shouldn't you be back in Echo corrupting my daughter?"

She wanted to point out that technically she was his daughter also, but that seemed too obvious a point to make. "Ashley's a big girl. She doesn't need my help."

"But you've made it a point to get between us."

"If you mean by letting her stay with me after you kicked her out, then yes, I guess I have gotten between you."

He stared at her with eyes as brown as a chestnut. It only pissed her off that they matched her color completely. "Your mother would be so disappointed in you."

The mention of her mother had Margot shooting out of her seat. "How dare you mention my mother? How dare you even pretend to know what she would have felt?"

"She would have expected better of you. And so do I."

"Oh, that's rich, *Dad*. How can you expect anything from a child you refused to acknowledge? Or did you deliberately wait until I was eighteen so you wouldn't have to pay child support?"

"It was your mother's choice."

"To work herself to the bone trying to support us and pay her hospital bills? I don't think so."

"Where's Ashley?" he asked. He'd never been able to answer even her simplest questions about the past and the part he played. He moved his head from side to side as he searched the deserted restaurant. "Is she with you?"

"No, she's not. I try to leave her at home when I hit the bar for an early drink." The bartender emerged from the back and handed her the takeout box of cake. She signed the tab with shaking hands and felt disturbed to realize the Judge hadn't budged. She stood trapped between him and the bar. "If you'll excuse me, please."

"I don't want you talking Ashley into anything. She's immature and spoiled by her mother's doing, and I can't have her wasting her life with some dead-end job at a coffee bar."

"You know, you're right. I've tried to tell her how much more she could make at a gentlemen's club, but so far she just won't budge. Must be more of your wife's doing."

Margot watched his grip tighten on the chair. "You're nothing like her, you know." It didn't take but a second to realize he was talking about her mother. "The woman never raised her voice to anyone and didn't have a sarcastic bone in her body. "I can't imagine where your foul mouth came from."

"Must have been from you, *Daddy*." She ducked under his arm. "I'll give Ashley your best."

# CHAPTER 24

Phil had spent hours in front of the computer working on CAD. His eyes were tired, and yet his body was wired from sitting still for so long. Rebecca had brought her lunch from home and Danny was back at the hospital. With his stomach growling and an afternoon appointment at Wyndham, he decided to take his chances and grab lunch at the club.

The bartender had just delivered his fish and chips when McBain sidled up beside him with a scowl on his face. "You tapped her, didn't you?"

"Excuse me?" Phil choked. He picked up his tea to clear his throat.

"Don't play innocent with me, Williams. Maggie was all over me before she left. Then I catch you two together and suddenly she's not interested?"

Phil carefully set his glass on the cocktail napkin with the club's logo. "Margot dumped you?"

McBain clenched his jaw and took a seat on the stool. "I wouldn't exactly call it dumping."

So they were dating. Damn. Knowing they'd been together, for any amount of time, really stung. "At least you accomplished your research."

McBain scoffed. "Hardly."

"What do you mean hardly?"

"I mean I never got past first base. One innocent kiss on the sidewalk, and then she shows me to the door. And I'm a great kisser."

Phil swallowed his gloating smile. "When did she dump you?"

"She didn't dump me!" He signaled to the bartender for a menu. "She said she didn't have any interest in seeing me again. And I blame you."

"Did she say something about me?" Phil asked.

"No, but I saw the way she looked at you at the airport. We hadn't even made it to the hospital before she was letting me down easy. What gives?"

So Margot dumped him right after they got back. He felt elated and ready to bolt from the club to her house when he suddenly realized he might have more competition than just McBain. Who the hell was with her the other night when he found her in her pajamas?

McBain snapped his fingers in front of Phil's face. "Hello? Anybody home?"

"Sorry. Did you happen to see Margot later? The night you dropped her off at the hospital from the airport? Around seven-thirty?"

He shook his head. "No. I haven't seen *Maggie* since she traded in prime rib for hamburger meat."

"You're an ass, McBain."

"And you sure are interested in your receptionist."

"Former receptionist."

"Details." McBain sipped from his water before slamming it on the counter. "I ought to fire you. I called her first."

"You can't call dibs on a woman. She's not a piece of candy."

"Says you. I've been working her for months. I even told you about her."

"You told me about Maggie. I didn't have a clue you were talking about Margot until we saw you at the airport."

"So you admit you tapped her?"

Phil shoved his plate away and looked McBain in the eye. "I didn't tap her, as she's not a keg of beer. But if she doesn't want to see you anymore, I don't see why I can't pursue her socially."

"Fine," McBain said with a sneer. "You pursue her to your heart's content. But learn from the master. If she didn't want a piece of this," he waved his hand from his head to his waist, "she's not going to give it up for you."

Phil had to bite his tongue to stop from admitting she already had. He wouldn't stoop to McBain's third-grade level. "I guess we'll have to see about that."

\*\*\*

In all the years he'd lived in the Lowcountry, Phil had never been inside the local hospital. He thanked his hearty Midwestern genes for never getting sick and felt a measure of Danny's apprehension just looking at the imposing brick building. He couldn't imagine having to visit a loved one in the sterile environment. He thought of Margot. She'd said she missed most of her high school football games because her mom had been in the hospital. She practically grew up within these walls.

Thoughts of Margot had driven him to the hospital to visit Kate and to dig for information.

He punched the elevator button to go up to the ninth floor. The nurse who greeted him at the nurses' station sat behind a large counter, typing into a computer.

"Which way is 943?" he asked.

She didn't even look up. "About halfway down the hall to your left."

He didn't move right away, but stared at the scrubs she wore under an ugly brown sweater. Puce.

He shuffled down the hallway, a vase of flowers in his arms, and gave a quick knock on the door with Flannery written on the white board outside.

"Come in," he heard her call.

Kate sat upright in the bed with wires extending from her huge belly to the adjacent machinery. Danny was in a recliner chair in the corner talking on his cell phone. Kate had certainly grown since the last time he'd seen her.

"Well, look at you," he said, setting the flowers on a table. She was still beautiful, with her dark hair pushed back from her face, but a little of her excited glow had paled and he could see the worry in her vibrant blue eyes.

"Phil," she said. "I was wondering if you'd ever show your face."

He looked around. "Not my usual stomping grounds."

"I wish it wasn't mine, believe me."

Danny stood up, phone to his ear, and patted Phil on the back before escaping to the hall to continue his call uninterrupted. Phil could tell from the tidbits he'd overheard there was a problem at one of the sites. Kate's eyes followed him to the door and then swung back to Phil.

"He's so stressed out," she said. "I'm just lying here connected to all these machines and he's up to his ears in work. I can't get him to leave me for more than an hour or two. I'm worried about him, Phil."

"He hasn't said anything about a problem."

"That was one of the contractors from Solitude. It's been one headache after another. You know him, you know how he gets when he's been cooped up inside for too long."

Phil certainly did know how Danny was when he couldn't work. He was like a caged bear. "I'll talk to him when he gets back, see if I can get him out to the site with me."

"I'd appreciate it."

"So are you here for the duration?" he asked.

She shrugged and ran her hands along her belly. "My labor has stopped for the most part, but my blood pressure is still too high. I'm afraid I might be in here for a while. I'm trying not to get worked up. I mean, the longer I'm here, the more time she has to develop, but I'm almost as stir crazy as Danny." She held her hands in the air. "But please, don't tell Danny I just said that."

"I won't." Phil was struck by how both Danny and Kate worried over the other. The minute one was out of earshot, all they could do was worry over the other. Danny was one lucky guy. Phil remembered how hard they'd fought to be together and knew luck didn't have anything to do with their happiness. "Did you say 'she'?"

Kate's smile bloomed as if someone had turned on a switch and she was lit from within. "It's a girl. She's a girl." She blushed. "We're having a girl."

"I thought you weren't going to find out?"

"We weren't, but after all this, I wanted to know."

"Is there anything you need, other than me getting Danny out of your hair?"

"Actually, there is one thing." She ducked her head and then looked up at him from under her lashes. "I hate to ask, but I don't want Danny running any more mindless errands when he could be getting some work done."

"Name it," Phil said.

"Teddy's driving Margot crazy."

Kate was going to make it easy for him to fish for information by bringing up Margot first. "I don't really have the best set up for a dog at my place."

Kate laughed. "No, silly, I'm not asking you to take him from her. For goodness sake, you'd probably let him loose on the highway."

"I would not!"

"Well, you'd want to." She took a sip from an enormous covered cup. "Teddy needs his crate. He's driving her crazy wandering all over the house."

"So you need me to get him a crate?"

"Not *a* crate. *His* crate. Danny's got it in the back of his truck. Would you mind running it over to Margot's this afternoon? I talked to her this morning and she said she'd be home by now. She had her test today."

"Sure," he said. She'd even given him an excuse to see her. "I actually wanted to talk to you about Margot."

Kate's blue eyes sparkled. "You did?"

Phil took a seat in the chair Danny had vacated. "Do you know if she's seeing anyone?"

Kate's lips twitched. "Not that I know of. Why?"

"Well, the other night when I dropped Teddy off, there was someone at her house. I got the impression it was a man."

"Oh. I honestly don't know who it could have been." Kate looked down at her belly and let out a big sigh. "To be honest with you, Phil, I think Margot is interested in seeing you."

"She totally blew me off the other night."

"I think she assumed you regretted what happened over the weekend. Sorry," she said with a definite blush in her cheeks. "She told me what happened."

Danny walked back in wearing a scowl. "Fitzgerald is pissing me off," he said to Phil.

"What is it?" Phil asked, trying to switch gears from Margot to work.

"He ordered the wrong windows for the model and the ones we need for the foyer are on back order."

Phil slapped Danny on the shoulder. "Why don't you run over there and take care of this in person? I'm up to my ears with the Wyndham project, or I'd do it myself."

Danny glanced over at Kate as if asking for permission. Phil felt embarrassed for Danny.

"Go," Kate said with her finger pointed at the door. "Check it out, make sure things are running smoothly, and if they aren't, then deal with it. I don't care how long it takes, I'm not going anywhere."

Danny walked to her side and leaned over her with his hands on each side of her head. "I don't want to leave you."

"Danny, please. I'm fine."

"But what if you have to use the bathroom?"

"There are nurses here to help with that."

"Baby…"

"Danny, go. I insist. I've got the books Margot brought over and I'm feeling a little tired. I'm going to take a nap anyway. I won't even know you're gone."

He sighed, resigned, and gave her a lingering kiss before straightening up.

Okay, Phil thought, it must be nice to have someone care that much.

"I'll be back soon," Danny told her.

"Take your time," she said. "I'm not going anywhere."

"I'll drop the crate off on the way."

"No," Kate nearly shouted. "Phil's going to take it."

Danny's head whipped around and narrowed his eyes at Phil. "Why?"

Phil shrugged. "I'm heading over that way." When Danny just stared, Phil said, "Solitude is in the opposite direction and I'll practically go right by Margot's house on the way to Wyndham. I don't mind."

Danny made a face at Phil and then at Kate. "Okay," he said. "Is it going to fit in your car?"

A dog crate? In his Mercedes? Yikes. "I'm sure we can wedge it in the trunk."

"I can break it down," Danny said. "It'll fit." He gave Kate one last kiss and rubbed her belly before heading to the door. "Ready?" he asked Phil.

Phil pecked Kate on the cheek. "You let me know if you need anything."

"I will," Kate said, her eyes huge. "And thank you."

"Anything for you."

"Get your lips off my woman and let's go," Danny said from the doorway.

"I can't help it if your wife finds me irresistible," Phil joked and tugged his tie into place. "All women do."

They walked to the elevator, past the nurses' station where three of them huddled in puce scrubs.

"So, daddy, I hear you're having a girl."

"Can you believe it?" Danny said as the elevator dinged. "What the hell am I going to do with a girl?"

Phil slapped his shoulder and squeezed as the doors opened in front of them. "Love her, man. Love her."

Danny looked at Phil and nodded. "I already do."

\*\*\*

Kate reached for the phone as it rang by her bedside and tossed the magazine she was reading aside. "Hello?"

"What are you up to?" Danny asked.

She tried to sound her most innocent. "What are you talking about?"

"Baby, I know you too well. You're butting your nose in with Phil and Margot. Don't even try to deny it."

The man was impossibly bright. "Fine. I may have asked him to take the crate to Margot's house. So what?"

"So what? Did you forget you promised me you wouldn't get in the middle of whatever's going on between them?"

"I didn't forget, and I didn't break my promise. I simply asked him to do me a favor. Come on, Danny. You know you'd rather check on Solitude than deliver the crate."

"Of course I would, but I'd also like to check on our dog."

"Oh," she said. Sometimes she forgot that Danny loved Teddy as much as she did. "Sorry. I should have thought of that."

"You were too busy playing matchmaker to think about anything."

"I'm sorry, but I can't help it. They're perfect for each another."

"Kate…" She recognized the warning tone of his voice. Danny hated to get involved with other people's personal business.

"Well, they are and you know it too."

"I don't know anything except what people tell me, which is too much. I don't want to know they hooked up over the weekend. I don't care."

"She's in love with him, Danny. Don't you want them to be happy?"

He sighed. "Of course I do. I just don't want to be responsible for them. I'm not responsible for them, and neither are you."

"I encouraged her to go away with him, so in a way I am a little bit responsible for how miserable she is right now."

"Which is exactly why you should stay out of it. Leave them alone to figure things out."

"I just thought if I could get them in the same room, they might be able to work things out."

"Whatever happened between Phil and Margot is their business. Not yours."

"I like Margot," Kate said. "She's funny and real and such a nice person." She straightened her arm as the blood pressure cuff egan to tighten. "You're the one who encouraged me to find women friends. Well, I've found one now and this is what friends do for one another."

"Kate, I don't want you to get worked up about anything, especially our friends love lives. Think about Faith."

Kate reached for her belly as Danny spoke their daughter's name. "I do, Danny. I'm so glad we found out. I feel closer to her already."

"Me too. She's going to a beauty like her mama."

"She's going to be strong like her daddy."

"I love you, Kate."

"Oh, Danny. I love you too."

"So you'll butt out?" he asked.

She chewed on her lip. She didn't want to lie to her husband. "I'll think about it," she said.

73

# CHAPTER 25

Margot couldn't go home. She could barely drive through the angry haze that wanted desperately to wrap around her heart and squeeze the tears from her eyes. She wouldn't let him bring her to tears. Not now, not on the day she'd reached a major goal in her life despite anything he'd ever done for her.

Without making a conscious decision about where she was heading, she found herself at the hospital walking along the familiar hallways to Kate's room. She felt comforted by the bright lights and sterile smells that were so much a part of her childhood. Her friend would ease the sting. Her friend would help her calm down and put the episode behind her. But she wasn't ready to tell Kate about her past.

"Hey," she said when Kate ushered her in with a beaming smile.

"How was the test?" Kate asked.

Margot blew out a breath, so relieved to feel her world tilt toward normal. "Good. It wasn't bad. I don't want to jinx it, but I'd be surprised if I didn't pass."

"Yeah!" Kate clapped her hands. "I knew you could do it. When do you find out for sure?"

"It typically takes forty-eight hours for the results to post, but I've heard some people call to verify their license after twenty-four. I'm sure I'll start obsessively calling tomorrow."

Kate cocked her head and stared at Margot. "What's wrong?" she asked. "Is something bothering you?"

So much for normal. She thought she could hide her encounter with her father. She thought just being around her friend would help her put the incident behind her. She must have thought wrong. "I…I ran into someone. He upset me, that's all."

"An old boyfriend?"

Margot chuckled. "Not mine, no. He's a jerk, and he said some things…" She shook her head and took a seat in the chair by the bed. She didn't want to give her father the satisfaction of ruining what should be one of the best days of her life. "I don't want to talk about it."

"Okay, but if you change your mind, I'm not going anywhere for awhile."

"Blood pressure still up?"

"Just a little too high. I'm trying not to get impatient. I want her to grow and get bigger and stronger."

"Are you glad you found out she's a girl?" Margot asked.

"Oh, so glad. Now I just can't wait to see her, to see what she looks like. Will she have dark hair like mine, light like Danny, or something in between? Will she be round and chubby or long and thin? Hair or no hair? Content or fussy? There are so many unknowns."

"And you thought you'd ruin the surprise."

"Silly, huh?"

"Have you named her yet?" Margot asked.

Kate rubbed the side of her belly. "Faith Marie. I was a little worried about the double F's, but Faith was the one name we agreed on."

"Faith Flannery," Margot said with wonder. "I love it." She spotted the laptop on the table in front of Kate. "What are you doing?"

"There's so much I haven't done. I wasn't expecting to spend the last few weeks in the hospital."

"I've seen her room. You've got it set up and ready to roll."

"I know," Kate said. "Thankfully that's done. But I don't have diapers or bottles or any of the little stuff I'm going to need. I feel bad asking Danny to get it because that baby store gives *me* a headache. He'd go nuts if I send him there for supplies. I'm ordering everything I need online and having it shipped to the house."

Margot pulled the wheeled table in front of Kate. "Need some help?" Margot asked.

"That'd be great—wait!" Kate flung her hand over her mouth. "You're supposed to be at home."

"I am?"

"I sent Phil there with Teddy's crate. I told him you'd be home this afternoon. You have to go home."

"What? Why'd you do that?" Margot's skin started to prickle with dread. Phil at her house? Today? Oh no. Please, she prayed, let Ashley be at work.

Kate flung her arms in the air. "You two are impossible. How are you going to figure out what's going on between you if you never talk about it?"

"There's nothing going on between us! We talked about it and I let him off the hook before he started making excuses."

"Off the hook? Margot, you shared something together. Something special. And I happen to know he doesn't want to be let off the hook."

"It was only special to one of us, Kate. To him it was just like relieving a pressure valve. The farther away we get from the weekend, the more I'm able to see what drove us together." She ticked a list off on her fingers. "His parents insisted we sleep in the same room, his brother—believe it or not—made us watch horses mate, and we spent Saturday night locked in each other's arms, determined to convince the town he wasn't gay."

"Gay?" Kate sputtered. "That's why he needed you to go home with him?"

Margot stared up at the ceiling. She just couldn't keep her big mouth shut. "It's a long story, and if he finds out I told you, he'll never forgive me."

"Okay…"

"I mean it, Kate. You absolutely can't tell Danny."

Kate closed her lips and made like a key locking with her hand. "Not a word," she said. "I promise."

"Wait," Margot said. "What do you mean Phil doesn't want to be let off the hook?"

Kate smiled. "He came here earlier to ask me if you were seeing anyone."

"He did?" Her stomach felt all light and tingly. "Why?"

"He said there was someone at your house the other night when he brought Teddy. He thinks it was a man."

"Oh." She'd wanted him to think it was a man. She'd wanted him to leave so she didn't have to explain about Ashley. "What did you tell him?"

Kate's eyes widened and she chewed her lip in a way that made Margot's stomach hurt. "I told him you were interested in him."

Margot felt like she was going to throw up. She brought her hand to her mouth. "What did he say?"

"He seemed surprised because he said you blew him off. I told him you thought he regretted what had happened between you last weekend."

"Oh my God. Then what?"

"Then Danny came in and he left."

"He went to my house?"

"I think so. Where are you going?" she asked when Margot bolted for the door.

"Home. I'll call you later."

***

Phil lugged the wire crate from the back of his trunk and carried it up Margot's porch steps. He'd pulled all the way to the back and didn't see her car in the drive. He didn't know whether to feel disappointed or relieved. How could she think he regretted their being together? How could he regret the most satisfying sexual experience of his life? Not to mention the fact that he'd been miserable every day since without her.

A rapid round of deep barks met his knock on the door. When he heard footsteps and the sound of Margot calming the dog, his heart rate sped up. She was home. They were going to get things straightened out. Today.

A pretty brunette answered the door, holding Teddy by the collar. "Can I help you?" she asked.

"Ahhhhh, is Margot home?"

"No, she's not."

Teddy began lunging at Phil, his tail wagging a mile a minute. "Hey, boy," Phil said to quiet the dog before he ripped the girl's arm out of her socket. "I've got his crate. From Danny."

"Oh," she said. "Okay." She backed up from the door and dragged Teddy with her. There was something about her that looked familiar, but he couldn't place her. "Why don't you just bring it inside? I'm sure Margot will know what to do with it."

Phil lugged the crate into the foyer and closed the door behind him. "This thing is pretty heavy. Where do you want it?"

"Ummm," she glanced around the living room.

In the afternoon sunlight, Phil could see Margot's touches everywhere. The simple denim couch was covered in colorful throw pillows. Her bookcases were crowded with medical books and thriller novels. Magazines were stacked haphazardly on her scarred coffee table. It was the kind of room that made him want to settle in with a good book and relax, not at all like his sterile living room at home.

"Maybe in the corner over there." She pointed to a spot beside the long brown panels framing her window.

He set the crate down and knelt to put it together, securing the metal edges with the attached hooks. He glanced up and studied her. There was something about the girl. When she picked up a mug of coffee, he realized where he'd seen her before. He attached the last hook and stood up to face her. "Don't you work at The Coffee Bean?"

She narrowed her eyes at him and lifted a brow. "Latte with skim and with a sweet treat to go? I knew you looked familiar." She held out her hand for a shake. "I'm Ashley Hennessey."

Hennessey? Hennessey? They shook hands as he continued to stare. Why did that name ring a bell? "So how do you know Margot?"

"She's my sister," the girl answered.

Phil rocked back on his heels. Sister? He distinctly recalled Margot saying she didn't have any siblings. "I...I didn't know Margot had a sister."

"Well," she said and gave a shrug. "Half-sister."

"Half-sister?" he asked.

She stared at him as if he were too stupid to figure it out. "Same father, different mothers."

It hit him like a punch to the gut. Hennessey. Judge Hennessey. The judge who was rumored to have fathered a love child with a waitress. Holy Mother of God! Margot was Judge Hennessey's love child!

"Your father is Judge Calvin Hennessey?"

The girl smirked. "The one and only, unfortunately."

"Margot is Judge Hennessey's daughter?" he asked aloud because his brain just couldn't make sense of what he'd heard.

"Yep. She's the infamous love child. And the lucky one if you ask me. Our father's a tyrant."

He nodded and stared at Ashley Hennessey. He could see it her now, the shape of her eyes, the full mouth. Damn it all to hell. "Okay, well, I've got to go." He walked to the door. "It was nice meeting you, Ashley."

"You, too," she said. "I'll tell Margot you stopped by."

As he got behind the wheel of his car, Phil only knew one thing for certain. He needed a drink.

# CHAPTER 26

Margot shoved the car into park and ran inside her house, ignoring Teddy's bark from the back yard. "Ashley?" she called. "Ash, where are you?"

Her sister sauntered in from the back of the house wearing cut off shorts, slippers, and a sweatshirt. "What set your pants on fire?" she asked.

Margot tossed her purse on the kitchen counter, shoved her hair out of her face, and took a deep breath. "Did Phil stop by here today?"

"You mean tall, dark, and sexy? Yes, he was by about an hour ago. I know him."

"What do you mean you know him?"

"He's a regular at The Coffee Bean. He likes our cinnamon scones."

No, Margot thought. *She* liked their cinnamon scones. "Damn it. What did he say?"

"Nothing. He brought Teddy's crate, which you'd think was made of gold by the way the dog acted. He set it up in the living room and left."

"Did he ask who you were?"

"Yeah." She opened the refrigerator and pulled out a can of soda. "I told him we were sisters."

Margot slunk back against the counter and covered her face with her hands. Oh no. "Did you tell him your name?"

Ashley pulled Margot's hand away from her face. "The gig is up for you, sis. He knows you're the love child."

Margot swallowed a gasp. "Tell me you didn't use that disgusting term. Please, Ashley, tell me you didn't tell the man I'm in love with that I'm Judge Hennessey's love child."

Ashley looked away. "Well, you are, technically."

"Damn it!"

"Since when are you in love?"

"Since forever!" Margot burst into the living room, spied the crate in the corner by the window, and groaned.

"What's the big deal?" Ashley asked. "That scandal is old news. I don't know why you're so embarrassed by it all. Jeez, if my mom can get over it, so can you."

"Excuse me if I can't get over the fact that my father cheated on his wife, lied about it for years, and didn't bother to acknowledge my existence until my mother was on her deathbed!"

"You know, he shit all over us, too," Ashley said in a low voice that brought Margot out of her hysterical fit. "He's an ass who likes to control people. My mom should have left him. I should have left his house years ago." She set her drink on the coffee table and put a hand on Margot's shoulder. "I doubt Phil even cares who your father is."

Margot sank into the couch and threw her head back against the cushion. "He cares," Margot said. "He won't be able to help himself."

***

Phil walked through the motions at Wyndham, making adjustments with the contractor, inputting tasks into his BlackBerry. He set Margot aside, tucked her away in a corner of his brain so he could get through the rest of his day.

It was after six when he arrived at the office. He unlocked the front, went through his messages at Rebecca's desk, and headed back to his office. He pulled the bottle of whiskey from his bottom drawer and poured himself a healthy shot in a tumbler he'd snatched from the conference room. It stung like fire going down his parched throat and only fueled his discomfort.

He turned to the computer and did what he'd wanted to do since Margot's sister had outed her as the love child. He did a Google search on 'Judge Hennessey, love child' and scrolled through the entries. One had a picture of Margot. At eighteen, pale, her blonde hair blowing wild in the breeze, he barely recognized her. She looked so young. She must have been scared. The accompanying story unfolded everything she hadn't shared. Hennessey's visit to the hospital, the reporter covering the hospital budget cuts who'd witnessed a confrontation between Margot and the Judge. Gossip, too scandalous not to share, spread all over the pages of the local papers.

He hadn't recognized her, hadn't really even acknowledged the event other than to feel disdain for the Judge and the girl and their pathetic two minutes of fame. At the time the story broke, he and Danny worked night and day to get their business off the ground. But it had stuck. He'd often used the Judge as a barometer of what not to do. Mistakes always came forward. It was best to stay under the radar with everything—business, women, life in general. No flash, no frills, just decent living and patience for the rewards of hard work. Well, he thought as he slipped out of his Italian suit coat, maybe a little flash.

Damn it, the truth felt like a betrayal. She'd lied to him about her past. But staring at her frightened face on the computer screen, he understood her so much better. She'd always guarded her life. Hadn't she been studying for her nursing degree the whole time she'd worked for him and he hadn't a clue? In that way, they'd been the same. Hadn't he hid his Midwestern farm boy past with fancy clothes and a foreign car?

He'd shown her his life, his real life, and she'd envied him. Now he knew why. But she hadn't shared hers. He swallowed the rest of the whiskey and pushed away from his desk. He found his ball in the corner of the office and paced around while his mind raced. She was probably home by now. She probably knew he'd come by. She probably knew her sister had told him the truth.

He tucked the bottle back in the drawer before he was tempted to have another drink and he couldn't drive home. The last thing he needed was for uptight Rebecca to find him asleep in his office wearing the same clothes from the day before. He needed to go home, maybe go for a run, clear his head. As he got behind the wheel of his car and let the cool breeze hit him in the face, he knew his heart was what hurt the most.

# CHAPTER 27

Margot scrubbed her face clean of makeup and crawled into bed. She was exhausted, but in a good way. They'd said it would take a week or more for her body to adjust to working nights. After her second night at the hospital, she'd certainly hit what one nurse had called the time zone wall. The room darkening shades helped to block out the sun's rays on another beautiful day. So far, she'd only been able to sleep for four hours at a stretch, but today she felt so tired, she felt sure she could sleep for more.

If she could just shut off her mind.

It had been a week since Phil had dropped off the crate and discovered her identity. She hadn't heard a word from him since. Things at Flannery & Williams were busy, at least that's what Kate had said both mornings when she'd checked on her before going home.

She tried not to care. Things at Flannery & Williams were always busy, and that had never stopped Phil from having a social life. If only she didn't know that he'd asked Kate if she were dating anyone. If only she didn't think they would have had a chance if only he hadn't found out about her father. If only, if only, if only!

Her eyes drifted closed. When Teddy sighed from his dog bed, she did what she promised Kate she wouldn't do. She tapped her hand on the bed and called him. He jumped up, wagged his tail, licked her face, and settled in beside her. She wrapped her arm around him and gave in to the tears that had threatened to burst free since she'd discovered Phil knew her secret.

The sound of her phone ringing jarred her from a sound sleep. She reached for her cell where she'd left it on her nightstand and noticed the sun's position in the sky. She'd been asleep for hours.

"Hello?"

"Margot, it's Danny."

"Hi." Margot sat up and rubbed the sleep from her eyes. "Wait, what's wrong?"

"Kate's in labor. She wanted me to call you. She's delivering the baby tonight."

She tossed the covers aside and bolted from the bed. "I'll be right there."

"There's no hurry," he explained. "The doctors don't want to stop her labor. The baby's lungs are fully developed, so they're going to let things progress naturally. It could be a while."

"Okay." She looked at her watch. It was after seven. "I'm on tonight at eleven. I'll be in before my shift." She sat on the bed. "How is she, Danny?"

"She's good. A little scared—we both are, but ready to meet our daughter."

"Me too. I'll see you soon."

She stretched, let the dog outside, and got into the shower. As the water hit her square in the face, she realized she'd probably see Phil at the hospital and the gnawing pain in her stomach began in earnest. She didn't think she could handle his cool disdain, not after years of friendship and one incredible night of passion. She'd resigned herself to the fact that they wouldn't have a future, but could she handle being shunned by him?

*** 

"Did you call Margot?" Phil asked Danny as he paced his office. Was it hot or was it just the direct rays of the setting sun as they streamed through the window? He yanked his tie loose and picked up his ball.

"Yeah, I called her. What's this about?"

"Nothing, I just want to make sure she'll be there."

"I'm done matchmaking for you, Phil. I'm going back in to be with Kate. The rest is up to you."

Phil blew out a big breath. Yes, he thought. The rest was definitely up to him. He dropped the ball, threw some papers in his case, and locked the office up tight. He needed a run, a shower, and a change of clothes before he faced the woman who may or may not have stolen his heart.

The maternity waiting area wasn't crowded for a Thursday night. An older couple huddled in the corner chairs, him dozing against the wall, her reading from an electronic book. A few twenty-something women sprawled in the chairs nearest the television. After spying Danny's dad and step-mom along the far wall, Phil took a seat next to them facing the entrance so as not to miss Margot when she came in. He couldn't sit still for long. He fiddled with his BlackBerry, flipped through a magazine, and looked at his watch a million times.

Where was she?

At a quarter to ten, he wandered over to the coffee machine in the corner. When he heard Danny's dad's baritone over the hum of the machine, he glanced around to see Margot in dull brown scrubs and tennis shoes. If she'd seen him at the coffee machine, he sure couldn't tell.

"I just checked on Kate," he heard her tell Danny's step-mom. "She's fully dilated. It won't be long now."

"How are they holding up?" his step-mom asked.

"Good, I think. Kate's a trooper. She's trying to deliver without an epidural. She'd always planned to have one, but she doesn't put any more stress on the baby. I think Danny would prefer for her to have some relief. He seems to be doing worse than she is."

He stepped next to her, his approach masked by the waiting room's carpet. "Margot."

He'd kept his distance on purpose. He'd needed to think, to breathe, to let everything settle in his brain before running off to scoop her off her feet. He wondered if his attraction to her had faded. He wondered if he'd exaggerated his feelings simply because he didn't see her everyday at the office. He wondered if she wasn't interested in him now that she'd earned her position at the hospital and her real life had started.

When she turned to face him, he knew the answer to every one of his questions.

"Phil," she said with a look of cool disdain.

Even with the scowl, she looked magnificent. She'd pulled her hair back into a ponytail. Tiny tendrils framed her face. Her eyes seemed golden brown in the fluorescent light and he could smell her perfume, something clean and subtle. He'd have given his last breath to see her smile at him just one more time.

"Congratulations on the job," he said. Everything he wanted to say died on his tongue as she stared up at him, her eyes huge and unyielding.

"Thank you."

She wasn't going to make it easy for him. He turned away from Danny's dad and step-mom and guided her to an empty corner of the room with a hand on her arm. "I was hoping I'd see you. As a matter of fact, I called Danny to make sure you knew Kate was in labor."

"I work here now, as you can plainly see. If you wanted to see me, Phil, you know where I live."

She was nearly shaking with anger. "I know you're mad at me."

She snorted. "I'm not mad." She looked at her watch. "But I do have to run."

He stepped in front of her and blocked her path. She looked up at him with narrowed eyes. "Excuse me."

When she tried to move around him again, he sidestepped and blocked her way.

"Phil," she said. "I have to go to work."

"You're not on until eleven."

"Yes, I know. But as the newest member of the team, I like to review the charts before shift change."

"I want to talk to you," he said.

She slapped her hands on her hips and cocked her head. "So talk."

"Can we sit down?"

She huffed out a breath and sat in a chair, gripping the arms in a white-knuckle grasp. Her feet tapped a hasty beat on the rug.

"I know you're mad at me because I haven't called you in awhile, but—"

"I know why you haven't called. I know you met Ashley and you figured out who I am." She snuck a look at him. "And as much as I want to hate you for it, I understand completely. I have more baggage than anyone you've ever met. I have more baggage than anyone *I've* ever met. And you hate women with baggage."

"I do hate women with baggage. I do try to avoid women with baggage. I broke up with Kelly because of her baggage."

She tried to hop up and he stilled her with his hand on her leg.

"End of story, Phil. I make Kelly Bristow look low maintenance. My baggage and me have to get to work. I'll see you around."

"Did Ashley tell you we talked?"

She whipped her head around to face him. "When?"

"A few days ago. I went to see her at The Coffee Bean."

"She didn't mention it."

"Good. I asked her not to." He let go of her leg when she relaxed against the chair and he didn't think she'd jump up and run away. "She's very protective of you."

Her lips twitched. "Are you sure we're talking about the same Ashley? Five-five, long brown hair, green eyes."

"One and the same."

"Well."

"She told me about your father, how he's treated you, how her whole family has treated you."

"I don't blame her mother for hating me," she said in a voice so soft he wondered if she were crying. When she looked at him, her eyes dry and cold, he recognized the spine of steel that had gotten her through years of being on her own. "I've never wanted anything from him."

"He's an ass," Phil said. When she slanted her eyes at him, he explained. "He's a member at the club. He treats the staff like dirt, lords over the place like he's the king and everyone else are his minions."

"That sounds like him. If it makes you feel any better, he doesn't treat family any better."

"I don't care if he's an ass, and I don't care that he's your father." He reached over and pulled her hand into his. "I've missed you, Margot."

"I know," she said. "You'll get used to Rebecca. You just have to give it more time."

Silly woman didn't recognize an honest plea for her attention. He couldn't blame her for that. "I'm not talking about the office, although I still don't care for Rebecca."

She stared at him, her expression guarded and weary. "What do you mean?"

"When we got back from Cash, I thought we were…I thought you and I would…I wanted to be with you."

"You did?"

"And then you took off with McBain."

"Me? You threw me at him as fast as you could. You wanted me to go with him."

"I thought you were…dating. The whole ride to the airport that morning I was trying to think of a way to ask you to come back to Cash for Thanksgiving. I'd forgotten about McBain."

"We weren't dating!"

"I saw you kiss him. You'd said you had a date and later that night I saw you and him kissing."

"Oh, well, that was just one date. And I didn't kiss him, he just kind of…" she twirled her hand in the air, "swooped in and caught me off guard."

"That's not what it looked like."

"Well, that's how it was. You know him. You know he doesn't ask, he just does what he wants."

"I also know you broke up with him."

"We'd actually have to be dating for me to break up with him, but I did tell him I didn't want to go out with him again."

"I heard," he said and cleared his throat. This is the part she might have a problem with. "And then I found out about Hennessey and I felt blindsided."

"I can understand that." She dropped her eyes and kneaded her hands in her lap.

"But once I got over the fact that you hadn't told me, that you'd in fact lied to me, I realized I'd have done the same. I did the same. I never tell anyone about my family."

"At least you have a family. A nice, normal family."

"True, although normal is debatable. And they like you."

She gave him a sheepish smile and a shrug. "Ashley thinks you're hot."

He looked her square in the eye. "She's not my type."

"No? An attractive woman from a wealthy Lowcountry family is not your type? Since when?"

"Since you."

"Phil…"

"Look, I just want to take you out to dinner. Spend some time with you. I'm not going to lie," he said, "I want to sleep with you again. I can't be around you and not want you."

He recognized the look in her eye; he'd seen it before in the moonlight. "I work nights now."

"So have breakfast with me."

"When?"

"In the morning. Come on, Margot. I know what you like. Something hot and sweet."

She held out her hand. "It's a deal."

"It's a sweetheart of a deal." He leaned over to kiss her and jerked back when Danny burst into the room.

"She's here," Danny announced with tears in his eyes. "Faith is finally here, and she's tiny and so beautiful." He rushed over to his dad and step-mom.

"Well," Phil took Margot into his arms. "Seems like a night for new beginnings."

"Yes. It certainly does."

He brought his mouth to hers in a kiss that tasted of home. He reluctantly pushed away before he lost his mind and backed her against the wall. He looked down at Margot, her eyes unfocused, a sly smile on her gorgeous lips. "You lied to me about something else, you know."

"I did?" she asked.

"You, nurse Manning, look incredibly good in puce."

She nuzzled against the crook of his arm. "Flattery will get you everywhere."

# EPILOGUE

Margot struggled to untangle herself from Phil's arms and legs. Even with his enormous king sized bed, he had to sleep on top of her. Margot didn't mind, but it made slipping out of bed difficult without waking him up.

"Ummm," he stirred and gripped her tight. "You're not leaving."

"I've got to grab a quick shower before my shift."

He shifted so that he lay atop her, pinning her hands above her head. "How about a different kind of quickie?"

"Phil, you're not playing fair," she moaned.

"I never said I would." He nipped from her jaw, down her neck, and lingered on her breasts. "When's your next day off?"

"Saturday," she managed through gritted teeth.

"Friday night, when we get in this bed, you aren't leaving until Sunday."

"Not even to use the bathroom?"

"You'll have to earn a pass."

"A test? I'm pretty good at tests."

"Speaking of tests," he said with a bite to her shoulder. "I've got one for you. Since you didn't come home with me for Thanksgiving and you won't get any time off for Christmas, my family's coming here for the holidays."

"Here?" Why did the mention of his family make her heart pound in fear? Maybe because she and Phil had monkey sex in their guest room and she couldn't quite get over her wonton behavior.

"Here."

"That's nice, but what's the test?"

"My dad's upset that I've never put a ring on your finger since our last visit home. He's convinced we've already consummated our relationship."

"Well," she said with a pinch to his ass, "he wouldn't be wrong."

"So…" He reached across her to the nightstand and pulled open a drawer. Margot's jaw dropped when she recognized the robin's egg blue box. "I'm going to need you to wear this." He opened the box to the most spectacular antique diamond solitaire Margot had ever seen.

"You want me to pretend to be your fiancé?" Her heart physically ached from disappointment. She'd thought, in the last few months, that they'd started building a foundation for a real future together.

"Nope. I don't want you to pretend." He slipped the ring from the box, grabbed her hand, and glided the rock over her knuckle. "I want you to say yes."

She felt sick with excitement. "Say yes to what?"

"To me. To us. To our life together."

"For real?" she asked. "You're not playing with me, are you Phil?"

"Oh, I'm going to play with you." He cupped her face in his hands. "But not about this. I love you, Margot. Will you marry me?"

He'd given her everything she'd ever wanted. "I love you, too. So, yes. It's a deal. And there's no backing out."

"We'd better seal the deal." He glanced at the clock. "You may want to call in. You're going to be a little late for work."

# ABOUT THE AUTHOR

Christy Hayes writes romance and romantic women's fiction. She lives outside Atlanta, Georgia, with her husband, two children, and two dogs.

Please visit her website at www.christyhayes.com for more information.

Made in the USA
Columbia, SC
27 October 2024

44755628R00121